Praise For

THE
Marshal's
SURRENDER

"Such an incredible story! This story had me on pins and needles throughout the whole thing. Filled with excitement, mystery and love. Gus and Noelle skirted around the love they felt for each other but in the end love will always win out. Great story! One to read over and over again!"

Amazon Reviewer: "Cinderella 7", 5 stars

"Seldom have I read protagonists so completely devoted to each other. The suspense was nail biting and page turning and is the best of the series so far. That is saying something because the two prior books also earned five stars."

Goodreads Reviewer: B.D. Mann, 5 stars

"Marshal Gus Rose captured my attention in "Maybe This Christmas" and I couldn't wait to read his story. This delivered... The story is well told. Both characters have a distinct voice. The wintry setting is the perfect backdrop for a smart villain to close in and gain the upper hand. I thoroughly enjoyed the Christmas feel - one disrupted December that builds tension - with safety and love on the line. I highly recommend reading this if you enjoy Westerns with family, community, a showdown, and a sweet love story."

Goodreads Reviewer: Sara Cardon, 5 Stars

"The plotting and execution of this book was exemplary. The characters were well developed as well as personable. I felt like I had known them all my life even the secondary a[nd] tertiary ones. I fell in love immediately with Gus and Noelle and was drawn more deeply into the story as I turned (tapped my kindle) the pages.

"I loved the suspense the author executed so well throughout the book. At times she had me sitting on the edge of my seat reading as fast as I could."

Amazon Reviewer: Cheryl Pompilii, 5 stars

A Peek Inside

"This isn't a good idea," he whispered.

"Are you…" She opted for light-hearted banter. It would be so much easier if this came across as teasing, particularly if he turned her away. "Chicken?"

"Am I *chicken*?"

"Hmmm." She stepped even closer, tucking her boots between his. Her shins made contact with his. Mother definitely wouldn't approve, but she had a point to prove here, and aimed to do it right quick. "I think you are."

A grin twisted the corner of his kissable lips. "Not smart, calling a lawman yellow-bellied."

"Prove it. Prove you're not a coward, not scared of what one little kiss awakened in you."

"Think that kiss awoke somethin'?"

"I do."

He leaned down, until mere inches separated his mouth from hers. The weight of his arms about her middle felt so darn good, so right. It would be so easy to close the distance between them, to initiate another kiss. She fairly salivated at the thought of pressing her lips to his.

"I'm no coward," he whispered.

"Prove it."

He shook his head. "I think it was an anomaly. A freak thing. Random like a lightning strike. You'd just been through an ordeal, and it was gratitude and relief speaking."

But he hadn't pulled away. His words issued a

challenge of their own—daring her to prove that kiss high in the mountain canyon, when she'd been nearly frozen and scared she'd spend a night in the forest in December.

"I was happy to see you."

"In that moment, you would've kissed anyone."

She raised one brow. "I might've kissed my brother on the cheek. But that kiss?" She leaned nearer, wondering if he sensed half the pull toward her that she did toward him. She'd never been so incredibly forward, but found she didn't, couldn't, regret it. "That was for you alone."

The light faded further, making it even harder to see his expression, the clarity of his eyes. Oh, but she wanted to.

He shrugged.

"You doubt me?"

"Prove it." His whispered plea was all the prompting she needed.

She touched her lips to his and found herself swept into a kiss as powerful as the first. Only this one had a sense of longing that was infinitely deeper.

This kiss promised a beginning.

THE
Marshal's
SURRENDER

THE Marshal's SURRENDER

Kindle ISBN-10: 1634380177
Kindle ISBN-13: 978-1-63438-017-1
Paperback ISBN-10: 1634380169
Paperback ISBN-13: 978-1-63438-016-4

eBook and Paperback Cover designs © 2018 by Kelli Ann at Inspire Creative Services:
www.inspirecreativeservices.com
Copy Editing by RVP The Man Editing:
https://www.facebook.com/RVPtheManEditing/
eBook and Paperback interior design by Kristin Holt.

THE *Marshal's* SURRENDER

Sheriff August (Gus) Rose is a one-woman man. Too bad the only gal he's ever loved is married... *again*. Even if he were ready to court someone new—*which he's not*—Noelle Finlay would be his *last* choice. After all, her brother stole Gus's bride-to-be last Christmas.

The holiday season evokes unwelcome memories and he's almost glad an unruly gang provides a distraction. But petty vandalism rapidly escalates to hanging crimes—and the marauding bandits have targeted Noelle.

With his reputation as a lawman under fire and his tattered heart tangled up in Noelle, he discovers he's not only capable of loving her... he'll willingly die to save her.

***He'll surrender his tattered heart...
and his life...***

Thank you to Kelli Ann of Inspire Creative Services. *Your work makes me look good!*

A Sweet Historical Western Holiday Romance
Novella (Rated PG)
Holidays In Mountain Home, Book 3

by

USA TODAY Bestselling Author

*The books in this series are loosely connected and may be
read in any order.*

To hear about New Releases, Special Sales,
and *receive a FREE novella,*
Sign up for Kristin Holt's Newsletter.

www.KristinHolt.com/newsletter

Note: Kristin is e-free

One

Mountain Home, Colorado
December 1900

A single choice held all the potential necessary to alter one's life. *Forever.*

Noelle Finlay's parents had learned that lesson the hard way. They'd lived with that knowledge for nineteen years...every day of her life. Everything had changed since the letter had arrived and she'd confronted her parents.

Her entire life had been a lie.

Reminders surfaced at least once a week, often daily.

A single choice.

Such as craving five more minutes in the

warmth of her bed before rising. Like waiting for fresh coffee instead of making do with brew that had been on the stove since early morning milking.

Like the decision to cut through the Kennedy place, to shave five minutes. Dawn lit the winter sky but had yet to crest the mountain peaks.

She never rode across the neighbors' property. She was a good girl, always kept to the roads, always left on time. Always arrived at Pettingill's Tailor Shop at the appointed hour, often several minutes early. She prided herself on being in the right place at the right time.

Perhaps it wasn't a single choice that landed her in the snare of desperate trouble.

Perhaps a series of choices led to the danger at hand.

She urged Buttercup a little faster across the field, surprised to see movement in the Kennedys' yard.

Ellis and Jennifer Kennedy were supposed to be away, visiting married children and grandchildren for another two days. Had they returned early? Good. Just that morning, Pa had taken note of the impending storm. His creaky bones always forecast weather with surprising accuracy.

She urged the mount nearer the house. She'd call out to the neighbors, welcome them home, and make sure they knew she was the trespasser. A welcome trespasser, given the Finlays had cared for Mr. and Mrs. Kennedy's animals while they were away. That quick stop at the house would cost her thirty seconds at the most.

On approach, fine hairs on her arms rose even as Buttercup raised her head, her ears forward. The mare's pace slowed.

"What is it, girl?" Fear tingled through Noelle's spine.

Trouble.

Her whole body flashed from overly warm beneath multiple layers of winter clothing to frigid, as if Buttercup had tossed her into the icy river.

Men.

Four of them.

And Hector Kennedy wasn't with them.

The rhythmic pounding of hooves upon frozen ground wasn't nearly muted enough by the several inches of powder that had fallen overnight.

They'd seen her, as surely as she'd seen them.

Worse, her gaze snared with one man's, suntanned skin pinked by frigid air. Light hair hung lank beneath a dark stocking cap, his beard more red than blond. The slope of his forehead, the curve of his cheek, the exact blend of green and brown in the hazel of his eyes...all permanently seized by her artist's eye.

He held her captive with that iron-cold gaze...and a butcher knife to the throat of Kennedys' milk cow.

This *was* the milker—she'd done Mrs. Kennedy's chores when she'd been laid up last summer.

This wasn't a standard winter's butchering. No block and tackle. No preparation to bleed the animal.

Wrong, *all wrong.*

He didn't live here—didn't belong here. Wasn't a hired hand. Dark eyes tracked her approach, never leaving her face.

She'd recognize him, this stranger, anywhere.

Bile burned the back of her throat and her pulse pounded double-time.

And just like that, she knew—just *knew.*

This must be the gang causing trouble on the north side of the valley. Never this close to home.

No, *no!*

She swung Buttercup away from the house, tapped her heels into the mare's flanks, and urged her faster.

But not quick enough to miss the man's rapid draw of knife across bovine neck and an arc of blood splatter the snow.

Run.

Panic jumbled her thoughts, collided and frantic.

Heading straight home, her first instinct, would be a bad idea. Yes, Pa and her brothers were awake. But no one was prepared. Few would be armed.

Just in case the bandits didn't know who she was—*yet*—or where she lived, she would *not* lead them to her family.

Town.

She must alert Gus.

He'd protect her. He'd protect everyone.

Bitter-cold wind tore the scarf from her head.

Her ears stung with frost as she leaned lower over Buttercup's neck and urged the mare faster. Hooves slipped on snow and ice.

Long seconds passed.

Shouting from behind.

Buttercup regained her footing and galloped toward town.

Noelle pushed the horse to run.

Wind zipped past. Her heart pounded. She risked a glance back, relieved to see the bandits hadn't followed.

At last, she drew near town. She navigated Main Street as fast as the treacherous roads allowed. Her pulse roared in her ears and the shakes had taken hold.

Smoke curled from the stovepipe above the sheriff's office. *Thank God.* Already there—she wouldn't have to push on and rouse Gus at home.

She swung from the saddle, and slipped on the icy boardwalk, nearly going down hard. She caught her footing and pushed through the doorway.

Sheriff August Rose met her at the threshold. He caught her by the upper arms.

An immediate sense of security stole through her, near this man who'd made them all feel safe. But she still couldn't catch her breath.

She had his full attention. Gray eyes the color of a winter's stormy sky searched her face. He waited for her to speak.

"Kennedys'. Took a shortcut—" she gasped, her gorge rising at the recollection of the ringleader's hazel gaze, devoid of humanity. "The Ruffian Gang—"

Gus released her, grabbed his coat and shoved his arms into the sleeves.

Dual holsters rode low on his hips. Two Colts.

He buttoned the greatcoat as she disclosed the rest. "Four of 'em. They *killed* the milk-cow. Timothy milked that cow not two hours ago."

Her younger brother had been alone at Kennedys' place for morning chores. Fear spiked, taking her pulse along with it.

"Round up the deputies." He pulled on protective gloves.

"Yes." Her knees wobbled like a newborn foal. "They're armed. A butcher knife. Rifles."

He nodded, grabbed a rifle from the rack behind his desk, and jerked the door open. Snow flurries drifted in, swirling, caught in the current.

The thought of Gus facing four—at *least* four—*alone*...

Her fateful decision had brought Gus, U.S. Marshal turned Sheriff, into the fray.

Lawman or not, culpability rested on her.

What if she lost him? "Be careful."

He nodded, grim. He pushed his battered Stetson low upon his ears.

She followed him out, grabbed Buttercup's dangling reins and mounted.

He ran for the shed where he sheltered his horse. Times like these, he apparently left his mount ready to ride. He swung into the saddle, and with the ease of a skilled rider, headed south at a run.

By the time Gus approached the Kennedy place, the bandits had cleared out.

He swore under his breath.

This time, the Ruffian Gang had gone too far.

Beau side-stepped and tossed his head, offended by the stench of hot blood.

What a *mess*.

A bit of vandalism, a broken window, burning down a long-abandoned homestead on the outskirts of Mountain Home had let him know trouble brewed. But *this*. This was altogether something else.

Still, Gus didn't know who they were dealing with, not even a name. Folks about Mountain Home had taken to referring to the bandits as 'ruffians' which lead to Ruffian Gang.

The violence was escalating, and fast. Gus didn't like it. Not one bit.

He'd skirted the house, checked the barn, determined the tracks of at least four horses heading south, further away from town.

He wanted to give chase but caution urged him to wait for armed deputies.

Why hadn't the Kennedys raised the alarm?

Acid churned in his stomach. With a pistol firm in his grip, he dismounted and crept to the house's door. He listened. Sensing nothing, he knocked quietly. "Sheriff Rose. Open up."

The door was locked. He knocked harder.

He strained to hear anything inside. If Mr. and Mrs. Kennedy had witnessed the violence in their yard, they'd be right smart to stay locked inside and pray the attack ended with the cow.

He strained to hear over the whistle of winter wind.

Nothing.

Hadn't he heard something about the Kennedys' daughter expecting a baby? With a quick scan of the yard, the horizon, and the certainty he was still alone on the homestead, he checked the barn. Chickens clucked. A roan mare kicked at her stall. But the wagon was gone, as were the matched pair of roans.

The Kennedys were out, probably had been all night.

Turning his collar up, meager protection against the wind, he snugged his Stetson down tighter and surveyed the bloody scene. Footprints jumbled, mixed, all around the steaming cow.

This could've been Noelle.

Bile rose and he nearly lost his breakfast. He'd worn a U.S. Marshal's badge for more than a decade. It'd been ages since he'd lost a meal over the sight of blood.

But the thought of that young girl, caught by a band of miscreants was enough to—

Gus halted, listened.

Mountain wind whistled past, distorting sounds, finally carrying the warning to his frozen ears once more.

Riders.

Coming in fast.

He ran for his horse, on the sheltering side of Kennedys' house, pulled his rifle from the scabbard, and took up a defensive position.

Within seconds, it became apparent he had nothing to fear.

Noelle had acted fast, alerted his pair of deputies.

Same as always with the Ruffian Gang, the law had arrived. Too late.

"Good fellow," Gus murmured in the horse's ear as he handed him over to the livery. "You did real good."

Beau flicked his ears and eyed Gus with condemnation. The faithful gelding had carried Gus more than twenty miles. First, past the nearest neighbors to ensure they'd not attacked the Finlays and others. No matter how hard they searched, they'd lost the outlaws' tracks, obliterated by drifting snow.

The livery boys would dry him off, tend his abused hooves, see him fed and watered properly. Beau deserved the best. "An extra bucket of oats."

"That'll be a dime, Sheriff."

Highway robbery. Gus found a slim ten-cent

piece among the coins in his purse and paid.

His pocket watch said what the gloomy, snowy sky couldn't—half-past twelve. Noelle would be at Pettingill's Tailor shop or in the house out back.

Two places he'd successfully avoided.

But this wasn't the time for bellyaching and he never shirked his duty. He drew a deep breath, steadied his ragged nerves, and reconciled himself to the task at hand.

He'd assigned the deputies to send the butcher out to the Kennedys', with at least one of 'em as guard. Until they knew the Ruffians had fully retreated, he wouldn't risk anybody's health.

He stomped his ice-crusted boots on the shop's boardwalk, his frozen feet burning with looming frostbite. The cold and wet had long since cut clear through his Union suit. Bells on the shop door tinkled as he let himself in. The store, much the same as a year ago, was still warm, orderly, welcoming, and well-appointed.

Noelle wasn't there.

Instead, two ladies manned the counter, both waiting on customers. No sense standing around, biding his time 'til he could speak to one of them. He tipped his hat in silent greeting and hurried back outside.

He bent into the wind to block the driving snow with the brim of his hat.

On his second knock, Luke Finlay opened up. "Gus. Come in."

Gus shoved aside every uncomfortable

thought Luke spurred. *Business*. Nothin' more.

The warm kitchen smelled of roasting meat and freshly baked bread. Coffee, too. Hunger gnawed at his middle—breakfast a distant memory. He'd heard Finlay had hired a cook and housekeeper. She had to be around here somewhere. So did Noelle.

...and Effie.

"Find them?" The aroma of Arbuckle's coffee intensified as Luke poured a steaming cup, wordlessly indicated it was for Gus, and set it on the table.

Gus shook his head. He pried off his frozen boots with Luke's boot jack and left them on a mat. He resorted to pulling off his gloves with his teeth. He'd be jiggered if he'd ask Finlay for help unbuttoning his coat.

He sipped scalding Arbuckle's. "Lost their tracks." Giving up and turning back had galled him. Rankled worse to know by nightfall, the whole town would hear 'bout it. He didn't like the idea of everyone jawing about what he had or hadn't accomplished.

He'd been a hero when he'd taken this job. He intended to stay in the town's good graces.

It was all he had left.

Footfalls sounded from the second story. Light, feminine.

Luke Finlay was one lucky man.

Gus rattled around his big cavern of a house, with rarely another soul about. Not what he'd wanted, not his plan, but there it was anyway.

He sipped coffee and shoved the longing away. All the wishing in the world wouldn't change things.

Upstairs, the baby cried. Soothing, motherly tones trickled down the staircase and more footsteps sounded directly above, as if the nursery were situated overhead. Made sense, given the rising heat from the stove flue.

What, the baby would be a week old now? Maybe two?

Images of blonde peach fuzz on the tiny bundle's head intruded so Gus concentrated on the heat pouring from the stove and seeping through the porcelain of his mug. "I figure Noelle came here. I need to see her, ask what she saw."

"Of course." Luke paused in the kitchen doorway. "I'll get her. You'll join us for dinner."

He wanted to sit at this table with Luke and Effie about as bad as he wanted to ride another twenty miles in a blizzard, chasing his own tail. But he nodded anyhow.

"Noelle?" Luke called from the bottom of the stairs.

An exchange of ladies' voices above, more baby fussing, and the housekeeper, Mrs. Turner entered, busying herself setting the table.

Gus had just drained his Arbuckle's when Noelle joined him in the kitchen.

Her plum suit, trimmed in black piping and black buttons looked mighty pretty on her. Would complement her naturally rosy color—but something was off. The Noelle he knew would've had plenty to say already. "You O.K.?"

She lifted one shoulder.

The woman's pluck had run off. As if the bandits had stolen her vinegar, her posture seemed to curl in on herself, like spring corn frozen in the fields, turning black and dying.

Always was a tiny little mite, but the girl looked like a stiff wind would knock her on her backside.

He hated heaping questions on her when she looked so fragile, but this couldn't wait. "I need details of all you saw. Nothing's too small. Nothing's insignificant."

"I know."

"Let's pray," Luke said, holding Effie's chair, "then talk business."

Gus found his attention straying to Effie's familiar features. A pang of loneliness sliced through him every time he caught a glimpse of her—and this was worse, *far* worse. To be here, in her house, *their* house, with Finlay living the life Gus had planned and waited for.

"Amen." Luke reached for the platter of roast beef, took up the carving knife and fork. He served his wife a slice.

Wife.

"I saw his face clearly," Noelle said in a watered-down shadow of her own voice.

Gus could've kissed Noelle for the ease and completeness in which she captured his attention and put it right where it belonged.

"Whose face?"

"The man with the knife."

Anticipation zinged through him. "Recognize him?"

"No. I know everyone in the valley, and many from surrounding areas. I've never seen him before." She sounded certain and oddly settled. For a woman who looked like she'd seen a ghost, she was awful calm. Maybe things were starting to go right.

"Describe him." A big scoop of potatoes—his mouth watered in anticipation. Hunger made his stomach burn. He snagged two thick slices of warm bread off another plate.

Noelle pulled a folded paper from her skirt pocket, opened it, and spread it flat on the table between them. A pencil-sketched likeness stared back at him, stocking cap pulled low against the cold. Prominent brow, deep-set and dark eyes, a nose that had been broken, and a pointy chin mostly disguised by a curly beard.

He picked up the drawing, stunned at his good fortune. "You drew this?"

She nodded. Without another word, she ladled gravy onto her potatoes and passed him the boat.

"You got a good look at him." This likeness would make the search *so* much easier. Somebody, somewhere, would identify the criminal from this picture. He'd show it around, commit the man's face to memory, get the deputies in on the search—

Luke put his arm around his younger sister's shoulders and squeezed her little fist where it lay beside her plate. "Yes, she did. She got a real good look at him."

Gus's stomach fell. Hard. Like he'd been thrown from a horse. His brains must still be frozen solid, 'cause the impact hadn't hit him, not until now. He clenched his jaw, swallowed a string of profanity.

Noelle's big, golden-brown eyes snared him fast. "And he—" She swallowed and closed her eyes. "He can identify *me*."

"Whatever it takes, Noelle, I swear I'll protect you." *No matter what.*

"You're done working in town. Finished."

"*Excuse* me?" August Rose was not her father nor brother. He had no right to tell her what she could or couldn't do, yet he ordered her about. If Luke hadn't left to escort Effie through the lot to the shop, and if the housekeeper hadn't gone upstairs with the baby, Noelle doubted Gus would speak to her like this.

He sat on a stool before Luke and Effie's blazing parlor hearth, his hands and feet extended to the flames. He hadn't so much as glanced over his shoulder, oh, but he'd definitely noticed her dissatisfaction. His broad, steady shoulders tightened.

"You'll stay at home. Where it's safe."

"I'll do no such thing. If I do anything, I'll stay here with my brother and walk all of, what, fifty feet? The shop is no more than twenty steps through the back lot."

In one fluid motion, he pushed to his feet, spun to face her. *Tall.* So very tall...and far too near. Heat blazed in the storm-cloud gray of his eyes.

She stumbled back a step or two before she caught herself in full retreat and held her ground. He might be the law, but he didn't scare her.

"You realize," he whispered, "they got a good look at you, as you said. You'll lead them straight to Pettingill's. To *this* house. To Effie..."

The timbre of his whisper constricted. He loved Effie, still loved Effie. Probably always would.

"...and the baby."

The barb sunk deep. The urge to remind him he wasn't her keeper melted like ice too close to flame.

He was right. Blast him. The *baby... Effie...* Neither stood a chance against the bandits.

Noelle loved her sister-in-law, and loved the baby. She couldn't blame Gus for considering their safety.

Her posture sagged, matching her deflating determination. "What, I'm supposed to lure them into showing up at my home, instead?"

"Yes."

"My parents, my little brothers—"

"And a passel of hired hands. Lots of eyes and ears. Trained guns."

She held his gaze, his intensity full of

dominance and irritation.

"I'll talk to my dad about this." Despite enjoying the idea of Gus giving two shakes about her safety, *noticing* her, it still rankled to find him so bossy. This wasn't at all the way she'd dreamed of him looking at her.

"Don't think I won't have a talk with him myself."

"If you must. Keep in mind, my parents support my decision to work in town. Effie needs reliable help. Christmas is around the corner. We have orders backed up—"

"As soon as I'm warmed up and dry, I'm taking you home."

He made her sound like a wayward child. "They won't expect me in weather like this. They won't worry—"

He took a step nearer, so close he loomed. His shoulders seemed to bunch as if he intended to spring.

"—they know I stay here when conditions are at their worst."

His big hands gripped her shoulders. Her knees nearly turned to water. His hold tightened and her heart kicked in response. This wasn't how she'd imagined it would feel to have his hands on her. She'd anticipated this moment far too often. His gray eyes, alight with passion of a different kind. As if he'd throttle her.

This near, the damp wool of his vest carried a lingering scent of tobacco. Despite the reason he stood so close, she wanted to touch him. She wanted to push up on her toes and thread her fingers through the curls so long they brushed his collar.

"Do they know the Ruffian Gang slaughtered a milk cow not two miles from their house? Do they know the Ruffian Gang got a good, long look at their daughter?"

She gasped. "You didn't go by the ranch, check on my parents?"

"We rode past immediately. No sign of trouble, so we pursued." He clenched his jaw, frustration hardening the lines on his too-handsome face. "I sent Deputy Murphy to your parents an hour ago, and he's likely still there."

"So my parents will know I'm perfectly fine."

He held her gaze. "It won't take much for them Ruffians to guess which direction you came from this morning."

Her fists clenched. Every bit of air disappeared from her lungs.

That house contained her *family*.

"If they decide you're a witness and can identify them—I want your family, the hired hands, everyone on that ranch to know trouble's a-brewin'."

With the stark realization came a wash of dread, sharp and quick. "I have to get home." She tried to pull away but his grip tightened.

"We ride together, Noelle. From now on, you don't go anywhere alone."

Three

An hour later, Gus faced Noelle's parents in the room they used as a ranch office. Small, tidy, and sparsely furnished, it provided privacy for their conversation.

Phil and Caroline Finlay already knew the details from Deputy Sheriff Elias Murphy. Their fears had percolated a good while.

They wanted Gus under their roof. Day and night.

"Two days," Phil repeated, "that's all I'm asking. Two days. Make sure we've done all we can to safeguard our daughter. We need you, Sheriff."

"You realize I'm responsible for the whole town, the whole valley. I'm as obligated to each of them as I am to you." He'd said so once already.

"Far as we know, no one in town has seen the bandits up close." Old man Finlay's attention rested on Noelle. Phil loved his daughter. Plain as day on his face, the way he softened and radiated affection, concern, and worry. He'd die for this girl. No doubt.

Gus fought the urge to rub both burning eyeballs. *Jumpin' Jehoshaphat*. Might as well tie his hankie to a stick and wave the white flag over his head. "I'll stay."

Both Mr. and Mrs. Finlay, maybe Noelle too, sighed in the kind of relief that made chills walk icy footprints up Gus's spine. "Me being here doesn't guarantee nothing's going to happen."

"But this is what you did as a Marshal, right?" Noelle slid forward, out of her mother's embrace. The two women had bundled together on the sofa before the hearth. Firelight warmed her flawless skin and danced a fiery reflection in her eyes. "You guarded people. Judges. Their families."

In his former life, that's precisely what he'd done. But this was different.

"You were good at it."

"Yes. I *was*."

But now, the Ruffian gang—well, shoot. Gus was in way over his head with those varmints running loose.

Noelle's smile struck him with the force of a baseball bat to the chest. Disorienting.

"Sir—" Gus cleared his throat and focused wholly on Mr. Finlay. "We'll work up rotations of men to guard the house, inside and out. Do what we can to protect your property, your herd."

"Very good."

Somebody knocked on the door and pushed inside without waiting for a response. Elias Murphy, who'd left for town thirty minutes ago.

What *now*? Gus pushed to his feet. "Deputy Murphy."

"Gus—we got us another attack. A bad one."

"*Deputy Murph*y," he emphasized, "Let's you and me talk about this outside."

"Doc Cheney's tending to Widow Boczowski." The kid's mouth ran, pell-mell. "No saying if she'll live."

Mrs. Boczowski? Just yesterday the widow had sent for Gus. He'd ridden out to her place, found her hale and hardy. Presumptuous, but hale and hardy.

"Irene Boczowski is my friend." Caroline Finlay stood. "I want to know what those miscreants have done."

"She's hurt real bad, ma'am." Elias seemed to recall his Stetson, for he yanked it off and spun it between chapped hands.

"What on earth happened?" Noelle clung to her mother. Firelight reflected off Noelle's dark hair and the graying strands of the older woman's.

"Them bandits burned down her house, ma'am."

Caroline gasped. "Was Irene burned? Is that why she's at Doc's?"

"Nah. She weren't in the house." Elias shifted from foot to foot. "Them varmints knocked her about. Broke her arm too. Gus, you gotta come on back to town."

"Sheriff Rose has agreed to remain." Phil Finlay stood, arthritic pains evident in slowed movements. "You two deputies have things in town under control, don't you?"

"Well, I figure we might."

"That's good. Thank you for delivering the message, Deputy Murphy."

The Murphy kid, barely twenty, took Finlay's statement as a dismissal, for he shoved his Stetson over straw-colored hair. "Yes sir."

The Ruffian Gang might terrorize Mrs. Boczowski again. At least one bandit had been near enough to break her arm. She'd likely seen his face. "You keep a close eye on Doc's place tonight," he ordered the deputy. "Doc and Mrs. Cheney'd appreciate it."

"I can do that."

"See you do."

Just as quick as he burst in, Murphy yanked open the door and whipped it shut behind himself. Footfalls sounded in rapid cadence down the floorboards of the hallway. Mere seconds later, the front door slammed.

Phil held Gus's eye. "The kid going to be all right out by himself?"

Gus considered all he knew about the bandits' patterns, pictured the crude map he'd tacked up on the wall in the jail. A sea of blue X's, dates, and penciled question marks swam but stayed put. He mentally added the cow at Kennedys' and the burn-out at Boczowski's. Like a snow-globe, bits and pieces swirled and caught the light, drifting in meaningless eddies.

"He'll be fine. The deputy's the best shot in two counties." He'd bet his reputation on it.

"What do we do now?" Caroline hugged her daughter close, the desperation in her question focused on Gus.

"Anywhere you go," he told Noelle, "I'm there." He held her gaze, recognized the temptation her nearness would pose. "You stay in my sight as much as is proper. When you need privacy, you have your mother or sisters with you."

She winced.

"I meant what I said. You go nowhere alone. I'm with you, always." He swallowed, his heart shifting painfully against his ribs. "Whatever it takes, Noelle, I swear I'll protect you."

Noelle shouldn't have been surprised to see Luke and Effie arrive shortly before supper, but she was.

When Luke had hugged her goodbye shortly after dinner and wished her a safe journey home to the ranch, he'd entrusted her into the sheriff's care.

Luke had said nothing about leaving the safety of town. He'd yet to take the new baby out of the house, much less all the way to the ranch.

Through the frosted windowpane, Noelle watched Luke leap from his sleigh to the snowy yard. He waved to three mounted riders. Bundled against the cold, she didn't recognize the men or their horses, but assumed they were friends from town. All three carried rifles.

An armed escort, a new baby out in the winter chill, a sleigh loaded with satchels, bedding, crates and trunks, and arrival just before dark. It all added up to a long visit.

Noelle loved her brother and sister-in-law. *Truly* she did.

But must they arrive *now*?

If Gus weren't still wrapped up in Effie, if he hadn't loved her half his life, Noelle *might* have had a chance.

The meeting with the hired hands apparently finished, because Gus and Pa came out of the bunkhouse, followed by her two youngest brothers, Dallas and Timothy.

Luke raised a hand in greeting then helped Effie down from the sleigh, the babe bundled tightly in her arms.

Noises in the house dimmed the conversation in the yard, so she saw rather than heard the exchange between Luke and Gus. Luke brought out a tube...paper?...from the sleigh and handed it to Gus. Luke said something to Effie, who headed for the house on Pa's arm.

But it was Gus who captured Noelle's attention.

She watched Gus trail Effie with his eyes.

Pain squeezed her heart a little tighter.

Despite the condensation and frost on the

window panes, despite the distance between Gus and the house, she fancied she saw more than longing on his face.

He didn't seem happy Luke and his family had arrived.

Seeing Luke and Effie together had to hurt.

Noelle watched a few minutes more as Gus and Luke unloaded the sleigh, unhitched the team, led them into the barn, and stowed the sleigh. It couldn't be easy for Luke to bring his wife and daughter to the house, considering Gus might be here.

But Luke, by nature, would be worried about his wife, baby, and aging parents. He'd worry about Noelle, too. This was about safety in numbers, not about the past.

"Noelle?" Ma asked, catching her unaware.

"Yes?"

"Who's out there, dear? You're most distracted. I called you twice."

"It's Luke. He brought Effie and the baby. I think they've come to stay."

"Good. That's good."

No, it wasn't, but Noelle wouldn't argue the point.

"Mix up two pans of cornbread, will you?" Ma wiped her hands on her apron and headed to the back porch to greet Effie.

Noelle busied herself with the cornbread. She greeted Effie warmly, kissed the babe on her forehead, and slid the pans into the oven just as the men came in to wash their hands.

Talk focused on the rotating schedule of night watch, including breaking the ice on the herd's troughs, pitching hay, and guard duties.

"You're as welcome as the flowers in May," Ma assured Effie, "as is my granddaughter." Ma had claimed the baby, allowing Effie to remove her coat and hat. "What will you do about the shop, so close to Christmas?"

"I don't know how long we'll stay, so I brought a few things with me to work on. Perhaps Noelle can help me here."

Noelle hugged her sister-in-law and employer. "You know I will."

"I closed the shop early tonight. I have three women tending the shop tomorrow. I left instructions for finish work and deliveries."

Noelle nodded, then busied herself setting the table.

The baby fussed. Effie took a seat out of the way and prepared to nurse her daughter beneath a blanket for modesty.

The men came in, tossing ideas about, answering Luke's questions, and Noelle's eyes were drawn unerringly to Gus. She couldn't help sensing the discomfort Gus and Effie must both feel—Luke too, certainly.

She'd so hoped the intervening year would lessen the pain. When would the torch Gus carried for Effie wane?

How could Noelle possibly compete?

She couldn't...not when Effie, an ethereal blonde, dimpled, and beautiful was in the same room.

Gus *loved* her.

"Take your seats, everyone." Ma told the young boys to slide around and take the seats in the back. "Luke, bring in the chair from the office, will you?"

"Yes, Mother."

When everyone had taken their seats and talk still focused on the Ruffian Gang, Ma clapped her hands, effectively silencing them all. "We've had quite enough talk of this for one night. It's supper time, and I want peace at my table."

Several seconds of silence passed. Pa chuckled. Luke nodded, agreeing with Ma's request.

Pa asked a blessing on the food. Ma and Noelle carried the big pot of chicken and dumpling soup to the table and ladled up servings. Noelle cut the cornbread and set the platter in the middle of the table.

"Pass the butter, please." Luke reached to take the butter dish from Gus, and passed it to Dallas.

The conversation resumed, but this time, the easy talk focused on plans for Christmas.

How could anyone make plans? Wouldn't they have to wait and see how things progressed?

Noelle blinked, realizing she stared at Gus...had been staring at him for several minutes.

Embarrassed, though no one seemed to have caught her mooning over the sheriff, she busied herself with her soup and a bite of bread.

She couldn't help but notice Gus ate his meal with ravenous intent. He seemed completely at home.

She'd long believed he stayed away because being near Effie meant too much pain over lost dreams. He'd been quite vocal over how he'd been in love with Effie half his life and still was.

Ma served seconds. The plate of bread went around the table another time. And Gus, much to Noelle's surprise, seemed completely indifferent to Effie's presence.

Could he be as comfortable as he seemed?

Was it possible his heart had healed? Could it be he no longer pined for Effie?

Sure enough, Gus ate without a care. He didn't so much as glance in Effie's direction.

How often had she imagined what it would be like if he came to call on her? She'd imagined him at this table, having supper with her family.

She'd not seen Gus and Effie in the same vicinity for a full year. A lot could happen in a year. Much could change, including Gus coming to terms with Effie's choice. He'd had twelve long months to accept the situation.

Perhaps Noelle was the one who believed him still attached to Effie when…could it be?…he wasn't as captivated as she'd feared.

"Mrs. Finlay?" Gus spoke to Mother, thank goodness, rather than Effie. "This is the best cornbread I've had in ages."

"That's Noelle's doing. Fine cook, isn't she?"

"Indeed, ma'am." Gus winked at her then, his

beautiful gray eyes twinkling. For her. "Well done, Noelle."

A blush started beneath the collar of her plum suit and rushed all the way to her hairline. "Thank you."

That wink had her seeing things in a most optimistic way. Did she dare confess her feelings?

Frightening as the circumstances were that brought Gus into her home, she couldn't bank on him staying longer than the two days he'd promised Pa.

This was her chance. Her *first* in the past year.

If not now, when?

Four

After supper, Gus took the map Luke had brought in from town into the office and shut the door. With the house full of people, he needed a quiet place to think.

He unrolled the map, turned it right-side up, and smoothed it open on the desktop.

He found a pencil and added an X and notation for the Kennedy farm incident, then much further north, the burning of Mrs. Boczowski's home.

He stared at the journaling of events he already knew too well.

What was he missing?

Deep rumbles of male laughter came from the front parlor. Floor boards sounded in the hallway as someone walked past. The clatter of dishes carried from the kitchen.

The noise of a full house distracted him in the way only a bachelor who lived alone could comprehend.

Never before had he had such difficulty piecing together the clues, discovering who the culprits were and what they wanted. So far, all he gathered were random disturbances.

The gang's attacks were on the rise and increasingly more violent. The worst both occurred today.

Doubt ached in the pit of his stomach.

What did it mean?

Understandably, a green lawman would be perplexed.

But him? He hadn't been bewildered by a case in years.

Embarrassing. The Ruffian Gang had to be laughing their patooties off.

Outside, winter wind swept past, needling the house with shards of ice. The wind tinkled against the window. He'd bet the gang wasn't camping out. Not in this weather. They had to have a hidey-hole. Somewhere warm and secure. Like this family home—snug as can be.

He imagined the Finlay's house was precisely what a family home was supposed to feel like.

Comfortable. Secure. Filled with love.

Precisely what he'd hoped to buy for himself when he'd spent his savings on Mayor Abbott's mansion.

What a waste.

A soft knock came at the door. Noelle entered and leaned back against the closed door. "Mind if I join you?"

He smiled at her. "Not at all."

She approached, but only halfway into the little room. "What are you working on?"

"Adding today's attacks to my map."

"May I see?"

"I'm not nearly the artist you are."

"No matter." She smoothed the corner of his map flat, took in the details.

They stood side by side at the desk, focused on the butcher paper.

Through her eyes, the notations must look a mess. Nothing was spaced to scale, nothing made much sense.

Standing this close, he couldn't help but notice what a little mite she was. Barely reached his shoulder. Slender too. Wouldn't take much to sweep her up in his arms.

She'd been lucky to be on horseback when she ran into the Ruffians.

Not for the first time, his heart squeezed with something akin to panic. He hadn't panicked, not once in all his years as a U.S. Marshal. He didn't like the idea of panicking now. Only old ladies panicked. Panicking was too much like a fit of vapors. Far too granny-like for a lawman.

August Rose did not panic.

She opened her mouth as if to speak, but turned back to the map.

He grabbed the desperately needed distraction. "Go on. Say it. I draw like a toddler."

She grinned. "That comparison never crossed my mind."

"Something's on your mind." Maybe she'd seen what he couldn't. "Speak up."

She opened her mouth again, but whatever it was, she couldn't make herself say it.

"I know. The Kennedy place isn't that close to the river. My scale's nonexistent."

That made her laugh.

He liked making her laugh. Especially after the day she'd had.

Maybe he could do something right.

"Tell me." He nudged her with his elbow.

"It's nothing." He might not be able to find the Ruffians, but he had no trouble noticing the trembling of her fingers. She tried to hide the shakes by clasping her hands together but not quick enough.

He ought to stay on task, but how could he, with her in the room?

"I'd say it's something. You're shaking. You want to talk about it?"

"Most of the occurrences have been on the north and east, haven't they? Does that mean they're hiding out somewhere on the north-east side of the valley?"

"Maybe."

"You don't think so?"

"I think that's not what's on your mind. 'Sides, I suspect they're focusing their attentions to the north and east in an attempt to lead us astray."

"Oh."

He faced her then, leaned against the desk, and stared her down. She wouldn't look him in the eye.

He wanted to touch her chin, turn her to look at him. But that seemed a little aggressive. The poor girl had lived through a nightmare. If she wanted time to collect her thoughts, the least he could do was let her think.

Seconds passed. The fire in the hearth crackled. The window at her back reflected the firelight, her slim figure dwarfed by his much larger frame. So tiny and defenseless. He could only imagine how threatened she felt that morning, watching the villains slit that cow's throat.

"I'm glad you're here," she whispered. "We're all glad you're here."

He didn't understand women. All of 'em in the Finlay household had already thanked him. 'Bout a hundred times.

Once seemed adequate.

What was he supposed to do besides keep repeating himself? "You're welcome."

She continued twisting her little hands into a knot. Whatever she had on her mind, she still hadn't said it.

Maybe she didn't like the shocking differences between their sizes. Maybe he scared her.

"You want to sit down?" He fumbled for the desk chair, realized it must still be in the kitchen where Luke had carried it for supper, like his mama asked him to. "I definitely want to sit down."

He opted for the sofa where Noelle had curled up with her mother just that afternoon.

But Noelle remained standing.

Good manners dictated he stand as long as she stood, but something deeper prompted him to stay right where he was. The poor girl was having a hard time spitting something out and having him towering over her wasn't helping.

"I...uh—" She gestured vaguely, her hand still shaking.

"If I knew what you were trying to say, Miss Noelle, I promise I'd do what I could to make it easier on you."

She giggled, nervousness shading the musical notes.

"I gather you're scared, and it's perfectly all right to be scared." Ladies had that privilege. Lawmen, though, were expected to be tough, immovable, granite in the face of fear. "Is that what you're saying to me, Miss Noelle? 'Cause it looks like you're saying one thing and meaning another."

Her cheeks pinked and she wouldn't look at him.

"Shoot. I didn't mean to embarrass you. My mother would tan my hide."

"No apology needed, Sheriff Rose."

"Call me Gus." She'd *always* called him Gus.

"Of course. Gus. I'll leave you to your work."

"Stay." The word tumbled out of his mouth without warning.

She blinked at him. "Why?"

I need you.

You need me.

Neither seemed like a good idea to say aloud.

"Something important hides on this map. I know it." He tapped his chest with his fist, indicating that elusive sense inside that told him plenty. "I can't make hide nor hair out of the Ruffians' pattern. Maybe—'cause you know the area well—you'll see something I can't."

She blinked, doubt lingering in her cinnamon-colored eyes.

"Maybe your artist's sense will be too offended by my crude drawing..."

Doubt fled as she smiled. A gift, that smile.

"...but maybe, just maybe, that artist's eye will see something I can't."

She nodded.

"Willing to stay and give it a try?"

"Yes."

The following afternoon, Gus walked through the Finlay ranch house, double-checking doors, and ensuring Noelle remained in the close company of at least two family members. Less than twenty-four hours since he'd agreed to Phil Finlay's demands, and already the walls were closing in.

"You're baking Christmas cookies," Gus asked Mrs. Finlay, "at a time like this?"

She didn't look up from her floured rolling pin or the sweetly fragrant gingerbread dough.

"Christmastime is special in this family, Sheriff. I will keep it as normal as possible." Her voice constricted, betraying tears she fought to contain.

He clenched his jaw and fought the urge to swear. He never did know what to do with crying women. He pretended not to notice, grabbed a coffee cup from the drainboard and filled it with brew.

Behind him, she plunked down her rolling pin. *"Those men,"* she enunciated with stark clarity, with disgust etching each syllable, "might terrorize, torch houses, slaughter animals—"

The woman was strung tighter than a granny's corset strings.

Not good.

"—but they cannot steal Christmas."

He sipped at the steaming Arbuckle's, regretting the casual question about baking Christmas cookies. Who knew this homey, warm, delicious-smelling kitchen was dangerous? He'd walked into a battle and hadn't even known it. He needed to skedaddle.

"And," she pointed a flour-dusted finger at him, "you'd be wise to do the same."

"Yes ma'am." What other answer was there, though he detested Christmas?

"Wash your hands." Caroline Finlay left no room for argument. "You and Noelle will finish cutting these cookies and get them in the oven. I'm going upstairs to lie down."

The older woman had already untied her apron and thrust it into his hands.

Oh, no. Nuh-uh. No way would he wear a frilly calico apron.

"Put it on." Caroline paused to wipe her hands on a kitchen towel.

Gus stood, an apron strap hooked over his finger, as if it were a live rattler. He needed to mask his distaste better, for Caroline saw right through him.

"You're intolerable, Mr. Rose—"

Him? She was the one ordering him about, her good mood long gone.

"—and this home needs more Christmas spirit." She gasped, clutched her forehead as if a headache pounded there. "And I'm *tired*."

Of that, he was certain.

He balled up the apron and tossed it onto a chair. "Go lie down. Cookies can wait."

She narrowed her eyes into the glare he imagined all—O.K., *most*—mothers fine-tuned long before their first child was knee-high. That look conveyed a whole lot of *don't you sass me*. "You're living in my house, eating my cooking, ensuring my daughter..."

And just like that, the woman's composure crumbled like her extraordinary butter cookies he'd enjoyed just last night. Her shoulders sagged. Tears welled in her eyes. Laughter lines about her eyes and mouth seemed to deepen and fill with the kind of anxiety only a mother could understand—a mother who loved her children with wholehearted devotion.

Not that he understood from personal

experience.

"I thank you for every meal, Mrs. Finlay." He held up both hands, as if gentling a terrified animal. Frantic women were dangerous.

He watched the starch settle in her spine as she rose to her full height...almost reaching his shoulder.

"This is *my* kitchen, *my* home, Mr. Rose."

"Yes ma'am. That it is."

"That is *my* blue-ribbon gingerbread on that cutting board."

He didn't dare glance at the confection, though it did smell mighty fine. He had the distinct impression this conversation didn't have a thing to do with that prize-winning cookie dough or even the cookies themselves.

"Noelle is *my* daughter."

The vehemence in her tone took him back. What did the woman mean by that? Of course Noelle was hers. Like mother, like daughter. Both had a gift for saying one thing and meaning another. He never did figure out what Noelle had tried to tell him last night.

He waited, sure this lecture had to be headed somewhere and he'd best hold on for the duration.

"She's been through quite enough, wouldn't you say? She needs normalcy, a touch of homemade Christmas joy, and I aim to see she gets it—you, too, Sheriff, 'cause it's plain to see you haven't had nearly enough reason to celebrate the season."

She had him there. He didn't care if

Christmas came and went without so much as a howdy-do. Let the flurries of the holiday pass him by without recognition. That would suit him fine.

"I know what you're thinking." Caroline stepped closer, the fragrance of vanilla and cinnamon clinging to her clothes. "And it must cease."

He tried not to flinch. This woman who knew too darn much, given her son, new daughter-in-law, and newest grandbaby played starring roles in his tragedy.

"It's time to put the past to bed." She touched his cheek. A soft, motherly cupping of his jaw, like he'd seen her do to express both concern and love for her sons, her husband, even a hired hand or two. The gentle touch shocked him down to his boots.

That touch gave her the too-intimate ability to stare him straight in the eye and he wanted nothing more than to look away and hide his soul from her penetrating gaze.

"You have far too much living left to do, August Rose, and watching you pining for might-have-beens breaks my heart."

His jaw clenched beneath her hand—he couldn't help it. What business was it of hers if he pined over Effie? He'd *never* act on it.

Effie was *married.* Completely untouchable. *Again.*

Really, did this woman think he'd stoop so low as to tempt Effie away from her husband?

"Careful—" He sounded a mite too fierce, so

he clamped his jaw, silencing the threat.

"Shh." She swept fingertips over his whiskered cheek, then patted his shoulder like every time she brought platters to the table and brushed behind one of her children. The woman showered love on her offspring and their spouses.

What would it be like to belong to her family?

What would it be like to *belong*?

The craving swelled, as if he could be hungrier for maternal affection.

Only, he surmised, because he'd never known a mother's love. And now that he'd lived beneath the Finlay roof for *one day*, he'd glimpsed what it could be like.

He clenched his jaw tighter, to prevent swearing up a storm and tempting Mrs. Finlay with her bar of soap. He wouldn't put it past her to mother him, too, lumping him together with her grown sons.

He couldn't help but smile, despite the warring sides within him.

"Go find Noelle," she ordered. "Finish the cookies. You're supposed to be spending time right beside her, to protect her. Remember?"

Oh, yeah. He remembered. He glanced toward the doorway that lead to the hall and staircase. He knew she was upstairs with her sisters, changing bed linens and sweeping floors.

Maybe she would like to bake cookies, rather than spend the morning in housework.

"What if they've already stripped your bed? What will you do then?"

"Nice try, Sheriff. I won't have a lick of trouble making up the bed with fresh sheets—I'll be done before you get the first tray of gingerbread into the oven."

Five

The first gingerbread cookies came out of the oven when Noelle's experienced eye said so.

The heady aroma of cloves, cinnamon, and ginger made Gus's mouth water.

But he couldn't keep his gaze off the woman as she slipped a spatula beneath each cookie and moved them to a wire rack to cool.

She looked cute in her mother's frilly calico apron. And a smart dark brown suit that showed off her figure to fine advantage.

And he looked ridiculous. Who said he needed an apron? This get-up, though simple and unadorned muslin, was still an apron. U.S. Marshals did not wear aprons.

Ever.

But Noelle had slipped it over his head, spun him around and tied it at his back. Those fleeting moments with her hands on him had stolen the fight right out of him.

If his deputies could see him now, they'd laugh him to scorn.

He'd never see the day when they didn't crack jokes about a cream-colored muslin apron, and the pretty young woman who'd crooked her finger and reeled him in.

He propped a shoulder against the door frame and watched Noelle work. She moved about the kitchen with an ease that captivated him. The mere homey sight cut straight through his good humor and stabbed his tattered heart.

His kitchen hadn't had a woman's touch since he'd moved in last winter. Yeah, he used it, just to rustle up eggs and coffee in the morning, but the spacious room had seen better days. He ought to sell it to someone who'd appreciate it. Use it, not shut a dozen doors and ignore all but two rooms.

Sometime in the past year he'd settled on the inevitable—he'd live alone and he'd die alone. He'd never marry, never have sons, never settle down like he'd once believed he would.

Just wasn't the life for him.

He'd spent a year bedding down in the housekeeper's bedroom just off the kitchen. He saw no reason to trudge up the stairs to the master bedroom past all those empty rooms he'd hoped to fill with children.

Why torture himself?

And *why* had Mrs. Finlay reminded him of his pining heart? He liked holding that betrayal close to his aching heart. After all, his heart was lost and he'd never get it back.

"Gus." She waved a dainty hand in front of his face, as if this weren't the first time she'd called his name.

Tired of the morose cloud hanging over him, he figured laughter was the best antidote. He caught both of Noelle's wrists in his hands and pulled her close. She came willingly into what might have been an embrace, had he not clutched her arms.

"I've got you now." He waggled his brows.

Her peal of laughter did interesting things to his insides. They seemed to rearrange themselves, tingling a bit too pleasantly as she pushed up on her toes and...?

"What are you doing?"

"You have flour on your nose."

"I do not." He probably did, but couldn't make himself care.

She giggled, a throaty, heated melody, reminding him of the finest brandy...and not sounding one bit like a girl. This young lady, this *woman*, was full grown, whether he'd noticed or not.

He'd noticed. Run him out of town on a rail.

He glared at her sparkling eyes. "Did you just attempt to *lick* flour off my nose?"

She wiggled her fingers, clutched close as they were to his chest. "I haven't the use of my hands."

That would be, of course, his cue to release her. But he found this play too much fun. He liked holding her close. "It'll just have to stay."

Mischief brightened the spark in her beautiful eyes. "I like the sound of that."

His stomach tightened. Her skirts brushed his pant legs, and the curves of her figure suddenly seemed way too close. He ought to make an excuse and edge away. He had a dozen reasons all ready to fire: he shouldn't ignore their surroundings displayed through the kitchen windows, her parents wouldn't approve, the next sheet of cookies needed to go into the oven before the fire cooled.

Instead, he found himself holding on. "Like the sound of...what?"

Her pink tongue darted between her lips, swept over the plump lower curve of her smile. "You'll just have to stay."

He couldn't wrench his gaze free of her mouth.

"You said, 'I'll just have to stay.'" She drew a deep breath. "I like the sound of that."

His brain seemed to catch on her words. *You'll just have to stay.*

He hadn't said that... Had he?

This woman, Noelle, may well be the *only* gal he'd spent time with—other than Effie, of course— who'd shown genuine interest in the man. Not the badge. Not the appearance of money the Abbott mansion gave. Not the glamour—unbelievable, but true—of his profession.

Her fingers found his chest, teasing,

caressing. Her touch skimmed over his vest and encountered the derringer holstered in the leather braces that held up his trousers. He expected her to flinch as she discovered his hidden pocket gun— ladies always did. But not Noelle. She seemed far more interested in exploring his contours.

Somehow, his hold on her wrists had loosened. His thumbs stroked her palms. As if he'd do anything to prevent her from pulling away.

In that moment, he couldn't see anything wrong with that idea.

Noises throughout the house reminded him they were far from alone. And this young woman wasn't his. Her parents, brothers, sisters—shoot, *anyone*—would take exception to the way she'd pressed her body along his. Not the most proper batch of cookies he'd ever baked.

"We ought to make some icing." Was that his voice? Sounded breathless, as if he'd *already* kissed her.

What would her father do if he overheard?

Her gaze remained locked on his mouth, her cue as strong as any he'd ever seen. She'd welcome his kiss. He half expected she'd kiss him first, given half the chance.

He liked the idea of her kissing him first.

Did a whole lot to boost a man's sense of welcome.

Without realizing he'd released one of her hands, he found his right palm cupping her cheek, his fingers thrust into her hair. He pushed deeper, cradling her head and wanting nothing more than one kiss.

Just *one*.

Before he could act on it, though, she pulled away, stepped out of his reach, and twirled toward the cabinets. She stretched up on her toes, treating him to a view of the long lines of her back and a peek at her shoe and ruffled flannel petticoats beneath the hem of her skirts. She took down a mixing bowl and opened a drawer for a whisk.

He scrubbed his hand, still tingling with her heat, over his bearded face.

What on earth had just happened?

Really?

She'd decided to take him up on the idea of making *icing*?

He wanted her kiss. Real bad.

And by the heat sparking in her golden-brown eyes, she'd toyed with him.

The *tease*!

He growled, low in his throat, flipped the apron away from his holsters, and stalked toward her. His hands hovering over twin Colts.

She giggled.

He kept his features in a mask of determined focus. A predator. A gunman facing his quarry at high noon on a dusty Wild West street.

She backed up a step.

He took a long stride in her direction.

Her laughter doubled and she plunked the mixing bowl down on the table. She tossed up both hands in surrender. "I give up, I give up!"

His boot thumped, and he could almost see

the imaginary dust plumes of that lonesome street in his mind's eye. He narrowed his gaze, pinning her to the spot.

So near, all he need do was reach for her. She'd willingly step into the circle of his embrace, tuck her head beneath his chin.

One reach.

Their gazes snared, and for the longest moment, he drowned in the depths of her eyes...and his broken, lost, hand-me-down heart rolled all the way over.

His heart, so long lost to Effie, had changed course. Abandoned the past and somehow let go.

Unbelievable.

Impossible.

Never once, not before, during, or after Effie's marriages had his heart longed for anyone else.

Until Noelle.

After supper dishes were washed, Noelle put on her scarf, coat, hat, and mittens. If she didn't find five minutes to clear her head, the crazy longing Gus stirred up would boil over.

Twice, already, she'd caught herself staring at him, basking in the joy of having him near.

Foolishly, impossibly, hopelessly pretending he was hers.

"Hold up, Noelle." Gus leaned a heavily muscled shoulder against the door. "You know you can't go outside. Not alone."

Light from the kitchen lamp spilled into the hallway. The slice of light revealed his aggravation.

"Must I take two sisters with me to the necessary?"

"I'd prefer you don't go out at all."

Grim determination showed in the set of his jaw and narrowing of his eyes. Those beautiful eyes, wholly focused on her.

This near, he smelled of coffee and tobacco, and lingering hints of gingerbread cookies. He'd eaten four cookies, slowly, as if maximizing the enjoyment of the run-of-the-mill dessert.

He'd loved the cookies. She'd loved watching him enjoy them.

She really needed a break.

From *him*.

Gus reached past her with a long arm to grab his coat from a peg. *Almost* an embrace. "If you're determined to go out, I'll accompany you."

"That's not necessary. I'll be less than five minutes."

He didn't speak as he donned his coat. How could she witness his stubbornness and still feel so drawn to him?

Once outside, she noted his careful scanning of the yard, the darkened space between the bunkhouse and barn, the path to the milk house. His attention was everywhere but on her.

Why was she entirely focused on him?

"I heard you arguing with your mother before supper."

She clenched her jaw and stuffed her hands

deeper into her pockets. The discussion hadn't really been an argument...

"You're fighting the bit," he told her, the base notes in his voice making her shiver. "Don't go and do something foolish just 'cause you're aggravated by lack of privacy."

"I'm not *fighting the bit—*" She halted, whirled to face him. She sucked in a deep breath of air so cold her lungs burned.

"I think you are."

Did the man *want* a fight? "What do you know about me, August Rose? Have you ever once stopped to ask, to open your eyes and really see me?"

"I'm asking now."

Her heart pounded as if she'd run around the pasture twice, carrying a twenty-five pound sack of oats. Every bit as foolish an exercise as this conversation.

"Suppose you tell me what has you riled."

"I don't need your counsel, Sheriff. *Mother* and I have things well in hand."

As if he'd forgotten his vigilant perusal of the property, he folded his arms, settled into his stance, and waited.

All puff and bluster and male posturing.

She could be every bit as aggravating as he. She mirrored his posture and waited him out. A girl didn't grow up with too many brothers to count on the fingers of one hand without learning a thing or two about how the male mind worked.

He smirked. "You want me to guess."

"I prefer we don't discuss it at all."

"That's not gonna happen. You're disquieted. I can't protect you when you're itching to run about like a chicken with its head cut off."

A most unflattering comparison. "I am not disquieted. Thank you for comparing me to poultry at the chopping block."

"What did you and your mama argue about, if not the plan for your safety?"

How much had he overheard? No sense giving away more than he already knew. Maybe she wouldn't tell him a thing.

But the thought of a shared secret, an intimacy between them, tantalized and drew her in. She wanted to tell this man her secrets, ask his advice, lean on his broad shoulders, if only for a little while—

No.

That wasn't quite right.

She wanted to lean on him more than just tonight, or this week.

Given the choice, she'd keep him.

That sole reason had led her to maintain the job at the tailor shop. The U.S. Marshal had shown up in Mountain Home seeking Effie, who'd bought Pettingill's Tailor Shop and ran the place, so he was in there on a regular basis. Noelle might have quit her job long ago, especially since the wedding. If Noelle stopped going to town, where and when would she see Gus?

She preferred the natural, easy, chance meetings. Not the contrived, over-bearing, constantly overbearing efforts made by Virginia and Belle. Anyone with a lick of sense could see those two chased Gus with intent to lasso him and drag him before the preacher.

Maybe Noelle needed to be a touch less ladylike.

But according to *Mother*, Noelle already was *most* unladylike.

Ladies do not stare at gentlemen, Noelle. You risk appearing as though you welcome inappropriate advances. With him staying in our home, your behavior must be above reproach.

The heated rush of anger, and double-helping of embarrassment at the unspoken accusation that Noelle had inherited unseemly characteristics—

The recollection stoked her aggravation. She raised her chin and met Gus's eyes in the near dark. "That was a private conversation."

"If you two know something you've not disclosed, you must tell me."

A woman was entitled to her secrets. Her secrets had nothing to do with the Ruffian Gang and therefore were none of Gus's business. "On my way to the necessary?"

"You don't need to relieve yourself. We both know that."

This man aggravated her past the point of endurance. She wanted to slap him. Or kiss him. Or maybe whirl about and slam her bedroom door in his face. Or hug him tight and never let go.

Every time she envisioned herself alone with him, her daydreams were never like this. Cold, dark, on the path to the privy, and voices raised in accusation.

Gus nudged her chin higher, the leather of his gloves butter-soft against her chilled skin. Oh, how she wished—like in her stupid imagination—to feel the touch of his hand.

She tipped her head back and looked up, up, to meet him eye to eye. He seemed ever so much taller this close.

With the snow-covered fields reflecting light spilling from windows in the house, barn, and bunkhouse, the cloudy skies seemed more white than black. Just enough light to imagine she could see her reflection in Gus's eyes.

This, she had imagined. A perfect moment when she consumed his attention.

He touched her back, wordlessly nudging her closer. Her heart leapt.

Was this that perfect moment? When he truly saw her as a woman?

Was he filled with affection, warmth, and love?

He'd intended to kiss her in the kitchen— she'd known it. But Mother had appeared in the doorway and that had set off the vocal battle before supper.

Could it be he *still* intended to kiss her?

"When were you going to tell me," he asked, "that Caroline Finlay isn't your mother?"

The moment his observations—truly, only a hypothesis—fell out of his mouth, he realized he'd gone too far.

Blame it on the roiling, desperate urge to solve the mystery of the Ruffian Gang.

Blame it on the burgeoning awareness that he wanted to know everything about this woman. *Everything.*

Blame it on Mrs. Finlay's blasted blue-ribbon gingerbread and her heated insistence that Noelle was *her daughter.*

Coupled with the heated discussion he'd overheard prior to supper, he'd be an unworthy lawman if he couldn't put two and two together and come up with four.

He did regret the sharp pain marring Noelle's

beautiful face. "I'm sorry."

He shouldn't have said a word, no matter the conjecture swirling about his thoughts. He didn't need to be right, not near as much as he needed...*what*?

To keep this woman safe?

To make this woman happy?

She jerked away, or tried to, but he held her fast. His arm at her back proved helpful in keeping her close. He slid his free hand around her for good measure.

He really shouldn't hold her like this.

He shouldn't.

Especially not with her mad at him.

"I *am* sorry," he insisted. "I shouldn't have said anything."

"Who told you?"

Fear colored her tone of voice. He recognized fear. Knew it intimately. Fear made people unpredictable. Made rational people do irrational things.

He didn't want to know what fear would do to Noelle Finlay.

"Nobody told me. Just saw what I saw, heard what I heard, and based on a life of fighting crime, I sort of—"

"You think my life is a *crime*?" She tried to wrest free.

He held on tighter. He must make her understand.

This wasn't the time or the place for this conversation. Not in the open, not with a thousand vantage points all the way around them where the Ruffian Gang could be lying in wait. He needed all his faculties. He ought to keep a sharp eye open. He should be listening for footfalls in the snow, a whisper of voices, odors that don't belong.

Anything but swallowed up in this little slip of a woman he couldn't ignore.

"Your life is not a crime. *You* are not a crime."

"But my parents are."

"Don't go puttin' words in my mouth."

"You're the one who asked that ridiculous question."

"Wasn't ridiculous, now was it?"

She fell silent, even as she stiffened. She knew. And it was true. What on earth had happened, *how* had it happened? Unless Noelle had started out a cousin to the Finlays—a double-cousin, with parents who were brothers and sisters to Phil and Caroline—'cause she looked so darn much like Luke, Dallas, Timothy, Gerald, Miranda—all of 'em.

The only question that remained...was Phil her father?

This time, he'd let sleeping dogs lie.

"No one knows about that, all right?" She slowly relaxed, the tension in her body waning like a dying storm. "If you have an ounce of respect for my family, if you care about me at all, you won't say a word. Not to anyone."

He felt no satisfaction, knowing his hunch had been correct. "I swear I won't divulge a thing."

"See you don't." All pleading had fled. The

steely woman before him was a spitting image of the cougar-like Mrs. Finlay in the kitchen. Like mother, like daughter. Noelle *was* her mother's daughter.

"If I ever tell you about—" She shrugged, the movement of her little frame reminding him how very close he held her. "If I *ever* tell you my family's secrets, if I *ever* bring you into the fold, so to speak, you'd better be in to stay."

In other words, he'd never know the situation, at least not from her, unless he and she...

She and he...

He cleared his throat.

The possibilities—the impossibilities, rather—she and him? Together? Him, married to the Finlays?

Effie, a sister-in-law.

Like the past twenty-four hours.

Effie and Luke had been in the crowded house, sitting at the kitchen table at mealtime, and he'd barely taken note.

He'd been too swept up in the warmth of inclusion and too focused on the dark-haired beauty at his side.

"O.K." He cleared his throat again. How could he possibly say this? "If you ever tell me all about it, I'll know."

She nodded, the movement jerky. Her little hands had taken fistfuls of his greatcoat—when had that happened? Why hadn't he noticed?

He figured lots of stuff went on 'round here he didn't notice.

That scared him.

"That's right." She pushed up on her toes, as if she would kiss him this time.

He drew in a startled, deep breath. Even in the frozen out-of-doors, he caught a whisper of her scent. Flowers and clean woman and spices from her baking. Longing for so much more nearly drowned him.

"If I ever tell you all of it," she confirmed, "you'll know you're mine."

Noelle couldn't sleep.

Not with the anxiety of the day heaped upon her already frayed nerves.

Especially not with Gus asleep in this house.

His presence ought to lull her to sleep with confidence and peace and safety.

Instead, he distracted her constantly. She'd heard him go outside for a cigarette, smelled the hint of tobacco clinging to the air. Few of her brothers smoked, and her father did not. The fragrance tantalized, lingered, reminded her *he* was here.

She tossed back the covers, pushed her feet into slippers and pulled on her wrapper. Warm milk. That would do it.

She made her way to the kitchen, slipping down the stairs and avoiding the squeaky fourth tread. A quick poke to the banked fire within the range, a hearty splash of milk from the icebox into a saucepan, and a dollop of brandy, a spoonful of sugar.

In the parlor, she heard Gus turn over on the sofa. Apparently, he wasn't asleep, either.

This was ridiculous, really. He hadn't needed to sleep here. Not with the army of Finlays, gun-ready, and keeping watch. Nothing would happen.

Old Duke lumbered into the kitchen, stretching his legs behind him. Poor arthritic pup.

"Want to go out?" Noelle rubbed the collie behind both ears.

Duke shook off her love-pats and nudged the doorknob with his nose.

"Hurry back," she whispered. "It's too cold to stay out long."

Bitter cold wind, carrying a drove of falling snow, swept through the open door.

She turned back to the stove, stirring her hot milk, grateful for the warmth of the fire.

The house creaked and settled, the wind battering the siding. Snug as a bug.

The milk steamed and she reached for a mug, poured the beverage in and blew over its surface. The first sip tasted like home. Warm, relaxing, and oh, so enjoyable.

Duke scratched at the back door. She set down her mug, claimed the old towel used to dry off the dog after his romp through the snow, and opened the kitchen door.

With her gaze trained at knee-height, fully expecting the dog's snow-covered coat, she barely caught a glimpse of dark trousers tucked into boots behind a curtain of heavy snowfall. In that split moment, fear registered, swift and cold. Freezing temperatures cut through her flannel nightgown and wrapper.

Two men—at least two—grabbed her by both arms. One shoved a cloth that stank of pungent medicine against her face.

She couldn't breathe.

Terror sank its fangs deep.

She fought.

Struggled, twisted and turned, bucked.

One of the men closed the door softly. So softly, no one would hear.

Her slipper flipped free.

Bare flesh sank in snow.

Where was Duke?

Why hadn't he barked?

Gus!

She fought to remain conscious, to wrest her face free of the cloying stench on that cloth, to connect a foot against her captor's knee, but awareness faded, scoping in until she had no peripheral vision.

They'd kill her.

Death stalked her, seconds from pouncing.

She'd die from exposure, if not a knife to her throat.

Why hadn't she told Gus she loved him?

Gus!

One man's face loomed. "Settle down," he whispered. "Nighty-night, sweet thing."

A full hour before the sun's first hint of dawn tinted the wintry horizon, the Finlay family discovered Noelle's absence.

Within seconds of a sister noticing Noelle wasn't safely tucked in bed, the entire household had woken. A desperate, feverish search yielded nothing but an unlocked back door and a mug of cold milk on the table.

August Rose had been a trusted U.S. Marshal. He'd guarded federal judges, protected dozens of them from threats, seen and unseen.

Guilt buried him, sure as an avalanche, crushing the breath from his lungs.

The Finlays had trusted him.

Noelle had trusted him.

And he'd lost her.

The fault was his.

Entirely his.

Gus stood outside in his shirtsleeves in the driving snow that had fallen steady and fast for six hours, obliterating tracks. The bandits could have gone anywhere or nowhere.

The Ruffian Gang must have waited for the storm, planned it, grabbed the opportunity. They had to have known the snow would delay retaliation.

Six hours since Gus had lain half-awake in the parlor while she puttered about the kitchen, heating milk.

He'd thought her safe.

He'd heard the door open and shut, heard her murmuring to the dog. Knew she'd let the collie out. Then in.

He'd fallen asleep.

Fool.

She hadn't let the dog in. No Duke. Had the faithful, aged dog followed her captives?

His heart wrenched. Pain radiated in sickening stabs. Fear, greater than any he'd known, screamed in his thoughts, jumbled and vindictive.

Temperatures well below freezing, the chances of her surviving the past six hours were nil. Not in a flannel nightgown, wrapper, and slippers.

He shook, violently, his body fighting to stay warm. Fighting for life.

He didn't want to consider the terror, the pain, the misery Noelle had suffered.

Six long hours.

The Ruffian Gang's escalating crimes showed their lack of conscience.

Guilt drove Gus to his knees in the snow. The frost stabbed deep, punishing, but not enough.

What were the chances she was still alive?

He deserved the cold and snow, stinging his skin and burrowing into his marrow.

An innocent woman, so full of life and vitality, who'd stood in this yard and reminded him what it felt like to care about a woman—

Had that been just last night?

Emotion strangled his throat, cutting off his air. He scanned the yard, a bleakness so severe he thought he'd succumb then and there.

A lump in the snow...big enough to be human? Why hadn't he seen it before?

He charged, fell to his knees. Paddled the snow away in huge swaths.

Encountered black and white fur. Frozen and caked with congealed blood at the throat.

The Ruffian Gang had slit a cow's throat, then a dog's.

What would they inflict upon Noelle?

Emotion overrode, choked, swelled, erupted in a scream of fury. He bellowed a second time—more animal than human. He'd never, not even when Effie's father had banished Gus and his pa far to the north, removing them from Effie's life with precision—had such helplessness overwhelmed him.

Eviscerated, he screamed until his throat was raw. "Noelle!"

Gus stood on shaking legs. His teeth chattered. Hands and feet numb, he stumbled toward the house.

Until they located Noelle, he would not rest, would not slow.

On the slim chance she was alive, he had to move.

He forced back the tide of emotion and dug deep for the level-headed lawman.

At the kitchen door, he stomped off clinging

snow. Fire shot through frozen feet.

"Sheriff?" Caroline, tears flowing down her cheeks, met him with a blanket.

Another time, another place, he would have been ashamed of all the woman had likely seen through the window. Him on his knees. Howling in agonized desperation.

He nodded at Noelle's mother, accepted a blanket he didn't deserve.

In the kitchen, Phil and the boys had stoked the fire in the range. They wolfed down plates of scrambled eggs and shoved toast in their mouths. Dressed for the weather, armed, they'd be ready to ride inside of two minutes.

"What we gonna do now?" Dallas, his first whiskers upon his chin, looked to Gus with unwarranted trust.

A dozen things needed doing, all at once. "Phil, alert the bunkhouse. Send 'em in pairs."

Phil nodded.

"Bring in your married sons and daughter and their families." Gus fought the shakes, struggled to get blood moving again and his body temperature up. He'd be of no use to Noelle if he couldn't think straight. "The women and children will be safest here. Tell the men to dress warm, arm themselves, carry food and blankets. Noelle will need immediate care."

"I'll go, Pa." Timothy, lanky, tall, as dark-haired as all the Finlays.

"No." Gus gestured toward town with a tip of his head. He opened the blanket to capture heat from the stove. "I need you and Dallas to head for town. Alert the deputies. Tell 'em what happened, and to spread the word. Folks there need to be prepared. Tell 'em to stay home, keep an eye out, help their neighbors."

"But it's Saturday." Timothy sought agreement from his parents. "A week before Christmas. Nobody will stay home."

Gus flexed his frozen toes in his wet boots, cursing the weather for the hundredth time. Tracking would be so much easier in any other season.

"They will if they're smart." Phil set his empty plate on the table and pulled on his gloves. "Anything else you want my men to do, besides bring in my family?"

"Yes." Gus's pride had taken a beating, and it'd be a whole lot worse once everyone knew. "Leave half here, armed and ready. I want them in and around the house, safeguarding the women and children. Send the other half—door to door. Warn the neighbors and enlist as many strong riders and straight shots as possible."

Timothy set his plate on the table with a thunk. "I say we ride. Time's wasting."

"I'd like nothing more myself, son." Gus understood. "We're outnumbered, best I can tell, watching this gang over the past month. I aim to change that."

"Dallas and I can start tracking."

"You going to do as you're told?" Gus stared the youth straight in the eye. The boy was nearly as tall as himself, several inches taller than his father. "Can I trust you to take orders?"

Tim set his jaw. A muscle kicked in his lean cheek. Seconds passed. "Yes sir."

"Then I hereby deputize you to act in capacity of Mountain Home's Sheriff."

"Deputy? Yes!"

Gus settled a firm hand on the boy's shoulder. "That means you do *exactly* as you're told. Understand?"

"Yes sir."

"Me too?" Dallas asked.

A quick glance at Phil and Caroline for approval, and Gus nodded. "You too. Now git. Ride fast but take care of the horses."

The snow made for treacherous travel and the boys knew it. A horse could fall lame too easily.

"Yes sir."

"One more thing." He scooped up Noelle's pencil drawing of the gang's leader. "Spread the word this likeness is posted at the jail house. Tack it up inside."

"I will."

"Be quick. We ride the minute you return."

Seven

From the moment Noelle awoke, her mind foggy, and a disgusting taste in her mouth, questions rattled about in her aching head.

She pulled the woolen blanket higher around her shoulders and fiddled with the end of her braid.

Gus searched for her, even now, with her brothers and brother-in-law, Noelle was certain. He'd follow, despite the storm.

Because the drug had knocked her out cold, she hadn't any idea how far out of Mountain Home proper they'd traveled. Hours? Longer?

Where was this well-tended, fully stocked cabin?

For all she knew, they'd left the valley altogether.

Eventually, Gus and his men would have searched each homestead, every abandoned dwelling, and they'd expand their search. They *would* find her.

Why had these monsters taken her?

Why had they bundled her in blankets, provided heavy woolen stockings, protected her from the elements?

Most importantly, *why* would this band of miscreants allow her to see their faces?

They *knew* she could identify them. That didn't bode well for her safety.

They'd kill her.

Why did they wait? She felt like a goose, fattened up for Christmas.

She wanted answers, *needed* answers. They'd not bound her, gagged her, nor constrained her—so she would speak.

"Why did you kidnap me?" She directed her question to the one they called Boss, letting her anger and frustration show.

He shrugged in a manner that screamed insolence.

"You had a reason."

He ignored her. Stringy, unkempt hair hung to his shoulders. Dark at the scalp but gradually lightened to a reddish brown at the ends, as if he'd spent much time in the sun. His full beard shone red in the lantern light.

"I saw you butcher a cow. So, what? That's life. People butcher cattle every winter."

But not like he had. Gus said they'd not taken

the meat. The monsters hadn't so much as hacked off a haunch to carry away.

The remaining seven men avoided her questions in one way or another. Two slept. One stirred the stew on the stove. The one she'd dubbed *Tall and Ugly* stared into the fire. Another took great care feeding another log into the hearth. So she focused all of her attention on the ringleader.

Finally, he spoke. "I have my reasons."

"Suppose you tell me why I'm here."

He eyed her then, watching her with sharp intensity. Something in those hazel eyes seemed...off. As if he weren't entirely sane.

Of course he wasn't sane. Only crazy people stole women from their homes at midnight.

"You're our guest." He spoke in a slow and drawn-out manner, as if offering an explanation to a dimwitted child. "Independent of that...incident."

He had good teeth. Straight, white, strong. Looked like he still had all of them. A rotten man shouldn't have good teeth.

"Independent of that incident," she repeated.

"That's what I said."

"I don't understand."

He eyed her. As if he had no intention of justifying his illegal behavior.

"How long do you intend to keep me?"

"As long as it takes."

"You do realize you kidnapped me from my home in the middle of the night. That's illegal."

He shrugged. "No matter."

"It matters to me."

He seemed to think that through. His expression softened as if he considered what his actions had cost her. "I suppose it does. No need to fret. We've treated you with courtesy, haven't we? Anticipated and met your every need?"

They'd fed her, kept her warm, escorted her to the privy—but only to ensure she didn't fall in her slick-soled house slippers. In two trips outside, she'd seen no familiar landmarks, nothing but dense trees, and a stubborn white winter sky withholding clues of north and south, east and west.

She wanted to argue that no, the bandits certainly did not meet her every need. Depriving her of freedom and worrying her parents...but risking his wrath? He could make her a whole lot *less* comfortable.

Would he toss her into the snow? Tie her to a tree, without the cabin's shelter or heat of the fire? She wouldn't survive the night. Even without bonds, in weather like this, she had no hope of survival.

"What do you want? Ransom? My parents aren't rich."

He shook his head, the barest of movements.

"A slave to cook and keep house? If you wanted a wife, this was no way to win a girl's heart." She heard the sass in her voice and wondered if he'd strike her.

She'd not seen Irene Boczowski, but conjured images of the woman's injuries sprang to mind. One of these supposedly solicitous men had beaten her. Noelle could not doubt their penchant for violence.

What was the point of treating her well, if they intended to kill her?

They *would* kill her. She knew that. Why else would they allow her to see their faces and hear them speak?

A wave of homesickness washed over her, poignant, deep, and strong enough to pull her under. Regrets, bitter and sharp stung deep.

She should have told Mother she loved her. Especially now, with the truth between them.

Caroline *was* her mother in every way that mattered.

She'd never have a chance to tell Gus that story. She'd thought she had time.

Time to make things right with Mother, time to share her secrets with Gus, time to claim him as her own.

They were supposed to have time enough and to spare.

"I want to go home."

He didn't answer, but the flatness of his eyes shifted. As if compassion existed in him still.

"Please." She hadn't intended to beg. But if it'd do any good, she would beg. She'd beg loud and long and hard. One tear slipped over her lower lid and tripped down her cheek.

"Once you've served your purpose. Not until."

Her throat closed, twisted tight. *What purpose?*

He must've seen the question in her eyes,

guessed what she would ask, had she been able. Heaven knew she'd asked a dozen questions in the past handful of hours.

"You're bait, Noelle Finlay. Bait in our trap."

Bait?

Quick on the heels of that unwelcome surprise came the realization that baiting a trap with her meant one of two things.

One: he had a bone to pick with her family.

Or two: this had something to do with Gus.

After all, Gus was the law.

She would not, *could not* allow them to use her to bait a trap designed to ensnare people she loved. She'd die first, but she'd face death fighting to save her family, and Gus.

Love for Gus, the man her heart had chosen, made her strong, resolute, determined.

"A trap?"

Madness darkened the green-brown of his eyes. "We aim to catch us a U.S. Marshal."

A long, desperate day in the saddle drained Gus of the last vestiges of hope. Daylight had faded through shades of gray and muted brown, leaving them to search by light of the waxing gibbous moon. The horses' breaths showed in clouds of white.

The abominable snowfall had finally stopped, leaving powder knee-deep in the canyon.

Treacherous conditions or not, he'd not quit

until he found her.

Hours earlier, they'd divided into pairs, searched the valley and surrounding canyons in specific grids.

Three parties of Finlays and three parties of deputies with men from neighboring ranches spread out.

Gus rode west with Cliff Cox, Finlay's hired hand. The younger man knew the territory well and was quick on the draw. He'd shown dedication far beyond the call of duty. Gus was glad to have him along.

The man's attention never wavered, constantly searching for any signs of smoke, tracks, anything.

Good thing one of 'em had their head on straight.

All day, memories of Noelle lingered in Gus's mind. Her quick smile. The sparkle in her eyes. Honesty in those beautiful dark eyes when she told him that someday she'd call him her own.

Was that why he couldn't separate the personal attachment from his role as sheriff?

Because he cared too much?

He'd had all day to think on it, and he'd arrived at one unmistakable conclusion. He did care.

Noelle was the only woman, besides Effie, who'd made him want to say wedding vows in front of God, nature, and everybody. Noelle had wrapped herself up in the shreds of his tattered heart. She'd sought shelter where no shelter was to be found.

Try telling *her* that.

Funny thing was, that pretty little gal, so many years his junior, snuggled up inside his chest and fit there. Like a glove. He not only wanted to find her alive—*please, God*—he wanted to keep her.

A flock of birds flushed from low-lying scrub oak.

Gus cleared leather in an instant, reined in his mount, his senses sharp and attuned to every sound and image, the slightest flicker of movement.

Something had spooked them, and he didn't think it was their approach.

The rush of flapping wings masked all other noise.

He motioned Cliff to a halt and listened intently.

A twig snapped, and his gaze swung that direction, Colt at the ready.

He peered through lengthening shadows, cursing the clouds that slipped across the moon. The trees were nothing more than dark, shapeless shadows. He could be staring down a bobcat and not know it until the cat sprang.

He'd learned to trust his senses, and his senses told him a man was in those bushes, watching, waiting.

He and Cliff were sitting ducks, in the open. Might as well know if they faced friend or foe. "Who goes there?"

One second stretched into two. Wind whistled past, depriving him of hearing anything that mattered.

Finally, the crush of muted footfalls sinking in deep snow.

Gus pulled his rifle from the scabbard. "Show yourself."

A huddled figure, shapeless in moonlight, separated from the copse of naked trees. The mass barely looked human. A legless, armless lump.

"G-Gus?"

Could it be this easy? His heart shuddered.

He dismounted quicker than a hiccup. "Noelle?" Had they finally found her?

Too entangled in her, every emotion engaged, he couldn't make himself wait. Couldn't ensure she was alone.

He sank knee-deep in snow, and shuffled closer, both weapons pointed at the sky.

"That you, Miss Finlay?" Cliff nudged his mount nearer. The tack rattled.

"Stay back, Cox." The lawman, somewhere deep in Gus's rejoicing heart, surfaced long enough to be the voice of reason. "Stay sharp. Keep guard."

"Gus!" She ran, or tried to.

He holstered his left iron just as Noelle threw herself into his arms.

The force of her colliding with his chest, coupled with a rush of relief—hot and vivid and desperate—nearly knocked him on his backside.

Praise be.

He hugged her close, burying his face in her neck. "Sweetheart, are you all right?"

"I'm c-cold." Her breath felt chilled against

his cheek.

"Miss Finlay?" Cox's voice wavered. "Where are the men who took you? They close behind?"

She felt cold in his arms. *So* cold.

Jarred by Cox's reminder of Noelle's captors, how desperately outnumbered the two of them were, he swept her into his arms and made for his horse.

Flannel. His hand brushed the damp, frozen flannel of her nightgown. Heavy woolen blankets, weighted by ice, slipped as she lost her hold. He made a grab for them and wrapped her up. She clung to him, tight.

"Ma'am? How long you been out here?"

"I don't know." Noelle's teeth chattered. "An hour? May-m-maybe longer."

"Can you find your way?" Cliff asked. "Back to them, I mean?"

"I don't think so." Noelle shivered, sounding so small and vulnerable. "I wandered. Hid. Lost my way a couple times."

"Miss, did they follow you?"

"No. At least I-I-I don't think so."

Good questions, but Gus wasn't a Marshal or a Sheriff just then. He was a man who'd *finally* located the woman he loved. And she was alive.

Relief seeped into his frozen body, overwhelming gratitude for the miracle of finding her alive. Frostbite was certain. He wanted to get her warm, safe, home. "Noelle—thank God—"

She kissed him.

A hard, sudden kiss—and nothing like pecks

on the cheek from wives of federal judges he'd saved from assassination. This was the kiss of a woman.

He couldn't help it. He kissed her back.

This kiss contained so much more than appreciation. More than acknowledgment and relief and celebrating life. This kiss made his blood run hot and quick. This kiss ignited something within him that he feared would catch fire if he weren't careful.

A jolt of connection zapped through him, singing along frayed nerves, a hot rush of awareness so keen it nearly blotted everything else out—the cold, the circumstances, and definitely the awareness that *this* girl was the last girl he should kiss. The last girl whose kiss should move him.

He couldn't explain the anomaly. No one's kisses—other than Effie's, but that was understandable—had moved him.

This kiss grabbed him by the throat and held on tight.

The press of her satin lips against his electrified him unlike anything he'd ever known.

For the first time in forever, a long string of Finlay family Christmas celebrations, Easter dinners, run-of-the-mill Sunday dinners...with Noelle beside him, Effie and Luke present seemed...nice.

Comfortable and a whole lot like home.

"Sheriff?" Cliff's voice came from a long ways off. "Miss Finlay?"

She broke the kiss. Good thing because he'd

lost the wherewithal to pull away.

"Take me home." She hugged him tighter, pressing her face against the muff wrapped around his neck.

"Yes'm." He whipped off that scarf and draped it over her head to cover her ears and cheeks, then wrapped it about her neck. He drew a deep breath of cold air to clear his head, pulled off his coat and insisted she put it on.

Astounding. Surprising. *Life-changing*.

He bundled up that kiss and everything that came along with it and tucked it safely against his heart. He'd take it out later, reexamine, and wonder.

A careful man would hold onto his runaway heart, call it back, nail it down if he had to. A cautious man wouldn't allow himself to fall in love so quickly, so deeply, so completely. Hadn't he learned how bad it hurt when a woman changed her mind?

Effie *had* loved him once. But even she had changed her mind. And he'd barely survived the devastation of losing her.

Noelle might think she wanted him. Fool that he was, he'd already lost his heart to her. Amazing, really, that it was even possible he could fall in love. He'd believed, utterly and completely, that loving anyone but Effie was an impossibility.

How would he survive when Noelle changed her mind too?

He forced himself to look away from her trusting face, away from the love shining in her eyes, to make sure Cliff had it together.

Sure enough, Cliff Cox watched for signs of bandits.

With one more quick check of their surroundings himself, Gus lifted Noelle into the saddle, then swung up behind her. He took the time to get her settled comfortably, as sheltered by his body and protected from the elements as he could manage.

She snuggled against him.

"All settled?" he asked.

She nodded.

He couldn't wait to send a messenger to town, to ring the church bell long and loud and strong—the agreed-upon message that Noelle had been found. "Let's get you home."

Eight

"Tell me," Gus said to Noelle at the breakfast table the following morning, "every detail. Nothing is insignificant."

By winter's morning light, Noelle's skin held a pallor. The shadows beneath her eyes were dark. Her skin picked up the gray hue of her wool dress.

He wished he had a chair beside her as his vantage point across the table allowed his attention to stray time and again to her lips. Thoughts of that kiss were never far away.

Her kiss had left his world spinning on an altered axis.

Astounding.

Yes, he'd kissed others—Effie hadn't been the only woman to know his kiss—but no one...*no one*...had ignited his blood in an instant.

Only Noelle.

"I saw eight men." Noelle's tone sounded oddly flat. "They were all in the cabin, and only left to see to the horses." Her gaze settled on Gus and remained here.

He wanted to shift in his seat. She scrutinized his face a good long while.

Did she like what she saw?

Heat flared between them. As if the fire from that kiss had only been banked overnight. She remembered too.

All around them, the family ate their breakfast, subdued and quiet. Phil had offered a prayer of heartfelt gratitude and thanksgiving for Noelle's safe return. The man hadn't spoken a word since.

The family seemed content to let Gus ask the questions.

Noelle looked at Gus, tipped her head in confusion. "They did nothing to hide their identities."

Fear skated icy fingernails up his spine.

In his experience, gangs did not leave witnesses. They'd murder an innocent rather than risk a hangman's noose. "Names?"

She shook her head in the negative. "Nicknames for some. Not all. They called the ringleader Boss. He's the one I drew after the Kennedy attack."

"You're doing well. Keep going."

"They drugged me. Some foul-smelling

chemical on a cloth they held to my nose and mouth. That's how they spirited me away without discovery."

His jaw clenched. *Premeditated.*

"When I came to, I was in a snug cabin, dry woolen stockings on my feet and tucked into a clean, warm bed. I suspect they wrapped me up...I wasn't cold." She paused as if reflecting. "It was so *odd*. They treated me with utmost courtesy. Food, water, warmth. Woolen stockings and blankets. Escorted me to the necessary—but only to keep me from falling on the ice."

When the lawless behaved in gentlemanly ways, they usually had a strong motivation.

Why batter Widow Boczowski yet leave Noelle unmarked? Why treat Noelle as an honored guest?

One would think they had two gangs in the valley, not one. But Gus didn't believe that—not for a minute.

He pushed those questions to the end of the list. He couldn't bear to think what they might have done to her. He clenched his jaw and vowed, for the hundredth time, to catch the gang and see them answer for their crimes.

"What of the surroundings?"

"Completely unfamiliar." The tender flesh about her eyes tightened. "I couldn't see the mountains. The snowfall was so heavy, the sky so white, I couldn't tell east from west."

He rested his fingertips upon her forearm. Touching her, even through many layers of wool, reassured...until she flinched.

Noelle wouldn't meet his gaze and he knew a moment's fury unlike any other. If they'd touched her, he'd—

"No." She blinked, moisture in her eyes.

"No—" No, *don't touch me*? No, *that didn't hurt*? He needed to understand women—*this* woman in particular.

"I see what you're thinking, Gus, and the answer is no. Not one fist, not one kick."

But that left myriad other assaults—

She grasped his hand tightly.

He wished she'd taken off her mitten first.

"And it surprised me. From the way they grabbed me from inside the back door, I anticipated the worst."

"Did they *touch* you?" He searched her eyes, at an utter loss for words. How could he ask an innocent, particularly *this* woman, if they'd—

"No."

Honesty filled her eyes. *Untouched.*

He searched her expression for any tell-tale signs of a lie, but saw none. She spoke the truth, *thank God.*

"They told me," she continued, her bold gaze holding his, "I was bait."

Jumpin' Jehoshaphat. Shock stole his wind.

"Bait in a trap set for *you.*"

Everyone ceased eating. Phil set down his glass of milk with a thud that reverberated through the silent kitchen.

Gus's heart thudded painfully. Not once, since the attacks began, had he considered the miscreants might want to entrap him. Why *him*?

Noelle looked to her mother, then father. Her attention settled on Gus once more. "A trap set to ensure you walked into their hands, I suppose. They believed I would be enough motivation for you to come."

Doubt undermined her statement. Had she escaped, fearing he wouldn't come for her?

Utter certainty forced his honest response. "I would walk into the fires of hell to reclaim you."

His statement reverberated with the power of an oath. A vow made before her parents, siblings, and God.

She nodded, her eyes lowered. Didn't she believe him?

He'd convince her, though he'd ensure he never had to. He'd safeguard Noelle with his life.

He wished they were alone so he could reach for her, and wrestled with the overarching question: Why?

"What reasons did they give?"

"Boss wouldn't say. Just 'catch ourselves a U.S. Marshal.'"

Marshal.

Not Sheriff. Priceless information...*if* accurate.

During his decade in the U.S. Marshals Service, he'd handled hundreds of cases involving threats against federal judges, and sent scores of men to prison.

Where to begin eliminating threats?

He should be grateful for the developments.

Any revelations brought them closer to apprehending the criminals.

"I don't understand why they'd want to capture you." Mrs. Finlay set a platter of piping hot biscuits on the table, then dished two onto Gus's empty plate. "Eat up. You must keep up your strength."

She pulled platters of bacon, sausage, and scrambled eggs closer. "Eat."

"Yes ma'am." He filled his plate, hungry beyond measure. The family resumed eating, and Gus's mind whirled through cases, but he kept coming back to one nagging, unanswered question.

"Noelle, tell me. How did you get away?"

She spread butter over a biscuit and reached for the honey. "I couldn't sit there, waiting for them to capture you."

He swallowed, humbled by her bravery. "Go on."

"I said I needed the necessary and hurried out. They figured I had nowhere to go, it was getting dark and I was hungry, so I'd return. They foolishly trusted me."

Eight armed men. Hardly believable they let a captive attend to her needs unsupervised. How many minutes could have passed before one or more of them came after her? Five, ten?

The snow had ceased falling. They could have tracked her, recaptured her within minutes.

More like it, they'd set it up. He'd bet his bottom dollar they'd goaded her into escaping.

Why?

What motive could they possibly have?

Had they waited at a distance, watched until she found her way to safety? Would they have intervened, had she been lost? Had they banked on her carrying the slim fragments of clues to him?

Why kidnap a woman when leaving a note would be a surer bet?

He watched Noelle eat her honeyed biscuit with a fork, his heart beating too fast.

The puzzle pieces would not fit, no matter how he turned them this way and that...until, with a sudden and sickening click, that new puzzle piece locked into place. He saw his sketched map in his mind's eye.

Every attack had one thing in common.

Him.

He had visited every damaged ranch, homestead, and person. Many were his friends.

With his heart pounding, he met the many pairs of Finlay eyes, watching him with concern.

All those residents in town. The deputies. The silly girls who brought him lunch and persuaded him to pay calls.

Were they next?

"Sheriff," Phil Finlay said, concern in his voice. "What is it?"

"The Ruffians are watching me." His head spun. Thoughts of where he'd been, all he'd done...

He needed to warn folks he interacted with.

Based on the dates he'd tracked on the map... "They've been observing me for two months."

He'd communicated with far more people in

those eight or nine weeks than had been targeted by the Ruffian Gang. Were they aiming to hurt the people nearest and dearest to Gus?

He wasn't close to Widow Boczowski. He'd been to her place *once*. How had the bandits known Irene had wanted an *arrangement*? In arrears, he could see her gussied-up appearance, the manner in which she'd taken his arm and walked him to the house, and the hour he'd spent declining her offer. A town sheriff couldn't take up with a mistress if he wanted to safeguard his reputation.

Nothing had happened.

This piece of the puzzle was the first to fit with absolute certainty.

He *knew* he was right.

The Finlays. Panic infused his worry. "By staying here, I've endangered you all."

"We don't know that." Phil didn't sound convinced.

The entire family remained at the table, Caroline and the boys, Noelle and her younger sisters, Luke and Effie—everyone—overhearing every word. Included in the conversation and decision-making...even if they didn't speak.

Despite the family gathered 'round, Gus took Noelle's hand and held it with reverence. "*I know.*"

"If you have endangered us," Mrs. Finlay said, "it's too late to change things. Don't you dare run off. We need you here."

He thought her statement through, but couldn't see the point. "They'll come for me, whoever the yahoos are. That confrontation must not happen here." He considered mentioning women and children, but knew the Finlays would not forget their most vulnerable members. "You won't be safe, no matter where I am, until I bring them to justice."

Mother Finlay rested a hand on her husband's shoulder. Patience and understanding mixed with her concern. "We trust you will."

There they went, again, trusting him when they shouldn't. Nothing about his efforts to bring in the Ruffian Gang had progressed as it should. He might be at it for quite some time.

He might not succeed.

Noelle squeezed his hand. "I'm in this with you. We'll work together."

He remembered the impact of her first sketch. Was it possible this precious, clever woman held the key to discovering the gang's identities? "Can you draw their likenesses?"

She nodded. Mother Finlay brought a stack of papers to the table.

"Thank you." Gus flipped through quality portraits of seven men. What a steel-trap of a memory, to save and recall the details when she'd sketched.

She'd added color, capturing hair tints and eye shades.

"Are they familiar?" Noelle sounded hopeful.

He hated to disappoint. "I don't know. I'll study these with care."

"Good." Father Finlay scraped back his chair,

pushed his empty breakfast plate away. "What's the plan from here?"

"I'll gather a posse." He'd ridden with townsmen on three separate occasions. Every time, the gang had disappeared like smoke, the posse had lost their trail, and all had gone home disappointed.

Things were different this time. Now he knew the bandits wanted him. Their escalating frequency and severity of attacks indicated they were ready for a showdown.

Timothy, who'd listened silently through the exchange shifted in his chair, making the wood squeak. "When do we ride?"

"First light."

Noelle's father rested one hand protectively on his daughter's shoulder. "Surely you mean the *deputies* will lead the posse. You, son, are staying right here, to safeguard Noelle."

"Yes sir."

Best way he could protect Noelle was to figure out who the men were, and what bone they had to pick with him.

The Ruffian Gang wanted *him*. The conflict wouldn't end until they'd had their chance.

Gus aimed to give it to them.

Word of Noelle's safe return swept through Mountain Home like a blast of cold air from the north.

While the deputies and a few other posse members were expected, no one anticipated that half the town would show up at the Finlay place in sleighs, on horseback, and on snowshoe, demanding Gus round up the Ruffian Gang and end the threats posed to the community.

The whole main floor of the Finlay house—large though it was—was packed with people. The mayor and his wife, along with their tease of a daughter, Virginia, stood nearest Gus in the front parlor. The most recently retired sheriff, Liam Talmadge, also flanked by his busybody wife and flirtatious daughter, Belle, stood like the other slice of bread, sandwiching Gus in.

Gus accepted a chair Luke offered and stood on it, to escape the girls and all the better to see over the crowd.

He wanted to be heard.

From his vantage point on the chair, he saw folks crowding down the hall and into the kitchen where he knew more townsfolk had gathered. The livery stable owner stood on the stairs with Gus's Deputy Sheriffs.

Gus put two fingers between his lips and whistled, long and shrill. The idle conversations ceased and he finally had everyone's undivided attention.

"Now's the time for the community to pull together, as the Ruffian attacks have escalated."

"What," Mayor Abbott stated in a confrontational tone, "are you *doing* about this, Sheriff Rose?"

"Two posses ride at first light. One to the north and one to the northwest—"

The mayor cut him off in a presumptuous show of good favor from the townspeople. Gus had already fallen several notches in their eyes. Apparently, support continued to wane.

"Why not today? Miss Noelle returned home last night, did she not?"

"We're gathering information and resources." He still had not identified the gang members.

"Waiting gives them time to strike!" A man, somewhere near the back, complained loudly. The voice was unfamiliar and Gus couldn't identify the speaker.

Chattering continued. Women whispered. This impromptu town meeting was slipping beyond his control.

"Silence, please." Gus waited for the hubbub to diminish. "Rushing will endanger lives. I'm not willing to risk our deputies without an adequate plan and necessary protection."

"What about the rest of us? Our wives? Our daughters?" The livery owner folded his arms over a wide chest in a combative stance. He was always among the first to criticize, but never rode with the posse and wouldn't contribute so much as a spare horse.

Gus planted fists upon his hips. "Exercise caution. Stay armed. In town, keep an eye on each other. Those on outlying homesteads—"

Noise erupted. Complaints hissed and boos followed.

He'd expected resistance, but not outright jeering. He'd not seen this kind of mob mentality since the Peterson trial back in '95. That had escalated, flashed in an instant. Six men had lost their lives—a situation he could not afford to repeat.

"Keep weapons handy. Check on your neighbors." All common sense. No way could he and his small band of deputies protect every last citizen. That's not how it worked out here, nor in cities like Hartford.

The volume rose, tempers on a short fuse.

The people were scared—and they should be.

"Bottom line," he shouted over the hubbub, "I can't protect all of you. Men, step up. Protect yourselves."

For the first time in his many years as a lawman, doubts larger than himself expanded, grew, and threatened to overwhelm. Even when green, he'd known what he didn't know and had superiors to turn to.

Now, he was alone.

"You're the sheriff."

"We *pay* you to protect this town."

"You're the law."

The clamor grew. More muttering and dissenting votes. Abundant criticism.

A soft hand touched his arm, distracting him from the rising tension.

Noelle. Smiling at him in her soothing way. She spoke, but her words disappeared in the din.

He couldn't hear, so he stepped down. The

space was so crowded, she stood indecently close, virtually in the circle of his arms.

She pressed up on her toes, her breath warm against his ear. "I'll speak. Let me handle this."

He hated allowing a woman to fight his battles and defend his honor. But he would not deny her this. He offered his hand and steadied her as she climbed onto the chair. She caught the attention of a few among the crowd and they shushed the others.

Noelle gazed into the faces of long-time neighbors and friends. Gus couldn't miss the disappointment flitting over her features. That disappointment socked him in the gut and left him winded.

One by one, the neighbors, friends, and folks who'd known her all her life quieted. She must've sought out a few particular people in the crowd, for he watched as her golden gaze flitted and landed, communicating plenty before moving on.

"Sheriff Rose," she said, certainty echoing in her voice, "*rescued* me."

She clutched his shoulder and her touch communicated more than a need for balance. She offered far more support than she took. Warmth seeped through his jacket, vest, and shirt, right along with the pressure of her little hand.

His heart slid sideways.

"He risked life and limb, and found me at dark, more than an hour's ride from home. No one expected him to keep searching, not in the dark. If he'd turned back—"

Emotion stole her voice. He settled a hand over hers where she clutched his shoulder.

"If he'd turned back, I would not have lived through the night." Noelle let that statement rest heavily over the group, let it sink in. "I trust his judgment. I trust *him*."

Gus couldn't help the swelling in his chest at her words. Amazing how her confidence in him made all the difference.

...to this temperamental crowd.

...to his battered self-worth.

A feminine touch settled low on his back— and Gus flinched. That wayward hand did not belong to Noelle. *Who*?

He glanced over his shoulder to find frisky Miss Belle Talmadge leaning close. "I'm rooting for you too."

He appreciated the sentiment, but her touch made his skin crawl. If he had anywhere to go in the press of people, he'd step away. She stood far too close.

"Not only do I trust him," Noelle continued, "I agree with his plan. He and my father discussed this at length. And as I've had the unfortunate experience of spending nearly twenty-four hours at the mercy of the Ruffian Gang, my father has a vested interest in their capture *and* in our family's continued safety."

The crowd listened to Noelle. *Listened*. And remained respectfully silent.

In that moment, against every notion he'd carried in his aching heart for fifteen long years, he could picture this woman, Noelle Finlay, in his home. In his heart. Building a life and a family with her.

Why had it taken a crisis for him to see what had been *right there*, for a full year?

Just beyond Noelle, flirtatious Miss Virginia Abbott met his eye and wanted, obviously, to hold his attention. Gus rolled his shoulder as if dislodging a pesky fly, but Miss Talmadge kept her hand on his back. Slowly, she dragged her palm lower until it rested on his waist.

He shuddered and nearly spun in place to manacle her wrists in irons.

No doubt she believed her parents couldn't see her forward behavior, and, with the press of bodies, no one else could, either.

Gus tossed a hostile glare over his shoulder. Miss Talmadge's eyes merely rounded with exaggerated, innocent surprise.

"Likewise," Noelle said, drawing Gus's attention once more, "I'm certain you feel the same way about your families. *Listen* to him. *Listen* to the well-prepared plan he fashioned. If we work together, we'll come through this safely."

Nine

Gus hadn't been so wrung dry since the day Effie had chosen Luke. What a slap upside the head *that* had been.

Today, with most of the town doubting his capacity to do his job, heaped with his own self-recriminations, this day ranked even darker than the miserable Christmas he'd said goodbye to the love of his life.

It'd take a miracle to get through this.

"Sheriff?" Miss Belle Talmadge touched his elbow. Even through his coat sleeve, her grip felt invasive, too much. Not at all like Noelle's touch.

The young woman had made a pest of herself over the last year. Initially, when she'd started bringing in picnic hampers filled with lunchtime meals and goodies, he'd been flattered. Just days after he'd lost Effie, he'd needed the bolster to his flagging spirits. The attention had quickly become a nuisance.

"Miss Talmadge." He turned back to searching the snow-swept landscape surrounding the Finlay home. He'd braced both arms wide, resting on the porch railing. He'd needed air.

Even now, some families piled back into sleighs, saying their goodbyes.

He ought to head out back and find a bit of peace and quiet, keep an eye on the periphery. In all the commotion of people coming and going, the gang could easily slip back in. Anxiety formed a knot in his belly.

"Sheriff, my parents and I wish to extend an invitation for you to join us for supper."

Of all people, this one ought to understand. "I can't accept invitations now. You understand."

"Well, you do need to eat." She stepped nearer until she stood unbearably close. "You and Daddy could talk through everything. He was sheriff for, well, forever."

"I'll pass. Sorry."

"Ah, Gus. You know you need Daddy's advice and direction."

She'd turn into a shrew if she didn't watch herself. "The case takes precedence."

She stuck out her lower lip, pouting in a way she must've practiced in the mirror. Pouting women had never been his weakness. He turned his attention back to the jumble of sleighs still hitched and waiting in the front yard.

"You haven't called on me in weeks." With her arm still about his waist, she snuggled up into his side. By darned if she didn't press her bosom to his arm.

Little minx.

He shrugged her off, but she wouldn't take the hint. "No, Miss, I haven't."

"Call me Belle."

"Thanks, Miss Talmadge, but no thanks."

She narrowed her eyes. "You'll feel better once this whole mess is over and done with."

He folded his arms, spread his boots, and pinned her with his gaze. Yeah, he'd feel better once the bad guys were on their way to Cañon City for terrorizing Mrs. Irene Boczowski, destroying her property, and kidnapping Noelle... but that feeling better wouldn't have anything to do with Miss Talmadge, who really wasn't lookin' all that appealing.

As if the attack of one young woman wasn't enough, the mayor's daughter—the former sheriff's daughter's partner in crime—exited the front door and joined her friend on the porch. The ladies linked arms and both looked at him with a mix of appreciation and disappointment.

"We have complete confidence in you," Miss Virginia Abbott confided in a stage whisper. "We have every confidence, don't we?"

"That we do."

Dragging her cohort along, Miss Talmadge drew nearer and traced her fingertip down the front of his coat, tracing the circle of one button after another.

He nearly cringed.

What would it take to rid himself of these girls' attention?

"You know, don't you, that if you had a wife to take care of you, trouble like this would be ever so much easier, right? The community would look more kindly upon you if you were a stable, married man."

This was the most blatant hint she'd dropped, to date, and he didn't see her easing up.

"Ladies, this is not the time." Nor the place. Anyone could overhear.

"Just think about it, won't you?" Miss Talmadge's finger still drew maddening circles on his chest. He wanted to step backward, out of reach, but he'd never been one to retreat. He stood his ground.

Behind him, the door opened and closed. Families bustled toward their waiting conveyances.

He kept his attention riveted on the two girls. "No sense thinking about it. Like I've said, I'm not the marrying kind."

"Bah." Miss Talmadge smiled, much too confident. "A fine man like you needs a wife. You need to bolster your credibility in Mountain Home."

"My mother said the same thing." Miss Abbott patted her friend's arm. "Just now, naturally. And earlier. Both. Married men are ever so much more trustworthy."

Gus rolled his eyes. "Excuse me, ladies."

Miss Talmadge grabbed his coat collar and he was too much of a gentleman to pull out of her grip. He raised one eyebrow and waited for her to explain herself.

"Do be careful, won't you?"

"Always am."

"It'll be ever so dangerous riding out tomorrow morning."

Guilt twisted in his chest. He wouldn't be riding anywhere. He'd be here, safeguarding the Finlay family. He didn't like the idea of drawing the bad guys in that way, but Old Finlay was right... it seemed the most productive way to end this thing.

Miss Talmadge's hold on his collar tugged him closer. What a *pest*.

"Something you wanted, Miss Talmadge?"

She preened. She did have a lovely smile, but not near as captivating as Effie's....or Noelle's.

"Why yes, there is. As you're busy with this dreadful case, you'll be so busy, I don't know when I'll see you again. Allow me to issue my invitation now. Without family at Christmastime, I just know you'll be lonesome. Mother and Father wish to invite you to spend Christmas Day at our home."

"That's kind—"

Miss Abbott stomped one boot. "Now wait a minute—we agreed—"

Gus held up both hands, effectively dislodging Miss Talmadge's grip on his collar. "No invitations. I'm not feelin' social right now. Too much work."

Besides, he wasn't in the mood to celebrate

Christmas. It'd be fine with him if the season passed right on by in its blur of white and snow and icy temperatures.

"—he'll definitely come to the mayor's Christmas Eve party," Miss Abbott continued as if he hadn't spoken.

"Precisely! It's my turn for Christmas Day. Fair is fair."

"Ladies, I'm not a hair ribbon you can take turns with."

The pair glanced at him but quickly turned narrowed gazes back on one another. Let them have their little snit. He wanted no part of it. "If I ever marry, mind you, there's only *one* gal on my list."

What had possessed him to say that?

He clutched, his chest tightening from the stark realization that he *hadn't* been about to claim undying love for Effie Scofield...he'd been about to claim Noelle Finlay was the only one he'd consider.

Amazing.

"Who?" Miss Talmadge stepped nearer, a sweet smile on her pink lips. The cold had made her cheeks pink, her eyes bright. Someone else would find her attractive, appealing. She batted her eyelashes in a coquettish manner some bloke would find alluring. Not him. He'd always been a one-woman kind of man.

The mayor's daughter laughed. The musical tones usually made him smile. She'd had him grinning more than once when she came by the sheriff's office to feed him.

But today, these two seemed more shallow, more desperate, their flirtations annoying—the flattery had long since died. He really ought to put an end to it. "My apologies, ladies."

"What do you mean—*apologies*?" Miss Talmadge split a glance between her friend and him. "Oh, I guess one of us will be heartbroken, won't we? There is only *one* of you, after all."

Miss Abbott blinked twice in rapid succession. "There's no sense spending Christmas Eve with one of us and Christmas Day with the other...if you've made your selection."

An evil part of him wanted to taunt them. The girls were like dogs, fighting over a bone.

"Well, Mr. Rose?" Miss Talmadge seemed awfully sure of herself.

The door kept opening and closing. More families and couples and individuals heading out. Amid the low murmuring of voices inside, he caught a hint of Noelle's laughter. Now *that* sounded like pure happiness. Joy. Unfettered.

Good.

Very good.

After all she'd been through, it just seemed right and wholesome and precious and it tugged on his heart.

He'd nearly lost her.

"*If* I marry," he said, even as the pair of unwanted young ladies stepped ever closer, leaning in to hear him, "I'll have none but Noelle Finlay."

From where Noelle stood near the front door of her home, she easily overheard Gus's impassioned statement. "*If* I marry, I'll have none but Noelle Finlay."

She'd heard him, plain as day.

Crystal clear. Unmistakable. Shocking.

Precisely what she'd wanted to hear.

Unbelievable.

Memories of his kiss, not ever far away, swept over her with the heat and voracity of a forest fire.

That kiss had seared her to her toes.

And made her crave more. *Far* more.

This proved the tides had turned.

She found herself grinning like an idiot. And shaking Reverend Gilbert's hand. Naturally, he and Mrs. Gilbert had joined the others for the impromptu town meeting.

"Glad to see you looking so chipper, Miss Noelle."

"Thank you, Reverend."

"Happy you survived your ordeal."

"Me too."

She strained to hear the rest of the conversation. What else was Gus saying to Virginia and Belle?

She was still smiling, ear-to-ear, when the last of their guests filed out half an hour later.

She found Gus on the back porch, smoking a cigarette and scanning the tree-line along the back of the house.

He glanced at her, nodded, and blew out a

steady stream of smoke.

Confident his feelings were now in her favor, she determined to grab the opportunity by both horns and run with it. He might argue with her, but that would all be for show. It was time to act.

If she'd learned nothing else through her ordeal, she'd realized time was precious. She'd regretted not telling him how she felt. She wouldn't wait—not now that she knew he returned her affection.

Even with her coat bundled up to her throat, her muff securely about both hands, and her hat pulled low, the chill wind circled about her wool stockings and chilled her bone deep. She doubted she'd ever be warm again.

From here, it was easy to see a lantern bobbing in the hand of one of the men, moving from bunkhouse to barn. She watched Gus track the hired hand.

Inside the house, dishes clattered in the kitchen as her mother prepared dinner.

Homey sounds.

Familiar music.

She'd desperately missed her family and the safety of her home. It was good to be back.

Gus drew deeply on his cigarette and blew the smoke at a sharp angle away from her.

She opted for the direct approach. "I heard what you said to Virginia and Belle."

He groaned.

"It's fine. Really." She couldn't help but smile at him. "If *I* ever marry, I do believe the only man

I'd accept would be you."

"Noelle—"

The tone of his voice made it clear he regretted his statement. A chill of uncertainty slipped down her spine. Had he only made such a comment to throw those flirtatious twits off his tail? Maybe.

Or maybe he'd meant it.

"Shh." She couldn't help but touch him. She pulled one hand from the warmth of her muff and slipped it down his coat sleeve to his wrist, bare inside his coat pocket.

Feeling daring, more certain of her reception than before, she pushed her hand into the warmth of his pocket, nestling it inside his.

A rush of delight tickled through her. Especially as the expression on his face clearly read hope mingled with anticipation... and a bit of disbelief. Really? How could he not see how much she loved him?

He squeezed her fingers, just once, but it sent a rush of excitement skittering through her. Oh, she liked holding hands.

But then he pulled their joined hands from within his pocket and released her.

Now *that* was a disappointment.

"I'm sorry you heard that." Gus dropped his cigarette butt and ground it beneath his boot heel. The lingering aroma of tobacco smelled good. It smelled like him. She could grow mighty used to it.

"I'm not."

"Listen—I shouldn't have said that."

"Was it true?" She held his gaze, refusing to be put off. "Did you mean it?"

Discomfort etched his strong features. The decision to placate settled in place. "I'm far too old for you."

"What? Six years? Seven?" Bother. What did a handful of years matter? They were both adults.

"Depends. How old are you?—if I might ask."

"Nineteen." Her birthday, Christmas Eve, would be here before they knew it. He needn't know she was technically only eighteen.

"A baby."

"*Excuse* me?"

A hint of a smile tugged at the corner of his supple lips, making her ache for another kiss. That kiss upon greeting had been beautiful, glorious—a kiss between a man and a woman. Age hadn't factored into that kiss.

"I'm too old for you."

"No. If you were my father's age, then maybe. You can't be more than three or four years older than me. That doesn't count."

"Noelle?" He fell back a step, leaned his hips against the porch railing and folded his arms—as if that would keep her at a comfortable distance. It would serve him right if she threw herself into his arms and kissed him again. She had half a mind to do just that.

"Hmm?"

"Love doesn't work out so well for me, and I'm certainly not ready to court anybody. I only said what I said because those two seem to have decided my period of mourning is over and it's time to go in for the kill. I apologize for dragging you into this."

She shook her head. "You're scared of the spark that flared between us. You're scared of that kiss."

He seemed to choke on his own tongue and held up a hand as if to command her silence.

"Admit it." She wouldn't back down— couldn't. Not when they finally had a chance. Why would she let a misunderstanding get in the way of an honest chance at happiness?

"No offense intended," he began, "but you were only happy to see me. That kiss—it didn't mean anything more."

"Balderdash."

"*Excuse* me?" He mocked her now, mimicking her vocal inflections and register, too.

She slapped at his arm, giggling even as he chuckled. "That kiss was something special. I think you should kiss me again."

Unmistakable longing flashed through his expressive gray eyes before shutters slammed closed. "Not a good idea."

She drew near, pushing boundaries, risking a great deal. If he refused her, if he pushed her away, if he *dared* make some ridiculous statement saying if he ever married, it would be to old spinster Harriet McCormick, she'd never live down the embarrassment.

It was now or never.

Her skirts swished against his trouser legs.

One more step brought the toe of her left boot into contact with his. He stiffened.

He smelled of wind and winter, tobacco and man. She stood too near for propriety, but it wasn't near enough. She took a leap by tucking her muff beneath her arm and pressing both hands flush against his chest. So many layers between her palms and him. She fancied she heard his heartbeat quicken.

She could stand like this forever, near enough to draw in the scent that was uniquely his. Savor the fresh tobacco on his clothes, in his hair, the sandalwood soap on his skin.

She ached to draw her fingers through his curls...were they as soft as they looked?

Before she knew it, her left hand crept toward his coat collar and a chestnut curl.

"Noelle—" He caught her wrists in his hands, halting her progress. His hands felt so warm, the connection of his flesh with her own so welcome. Her heart skipped a beat.

She met his gaze in the fading daylight, the gray seeming darker, stormier. She wanted to believe it was because she affected him. *Please, let him feel something.*

Behind Gus, here came Cliff, carrying two pails of fresh milk up the snow-covered walk and to the back door.

She nearly smiled at his concerted effort to ignore them, as if they weren't there. He set the milk pails, covered with tin lids, on the porch by the back door like always, then turned around and hustled back to the warmth of the bunkhouse.

Through it all, Noelle kept her gaze locked with Gus's and he kept her wrists trapped in his hands.

"This isn't a good idea," he whispered.

"Are you..." She opted for light-hearted banter. It would be so much easier if this came across as teasing, particularly if he turned her away. "Chicken?"

"Am I *chicken*?"

"Hmmm." She stepped even closer, tucking her boots between his. Her shins made contact with his. Mother definitely wouldn't approve, but she had a point to prove here, and aimed to do it right quick. "I think you are."

A grin twisted the corner of his kissable lips. "Not smart, calling a lawman yellow-bellied."

"Prove it. Prove you're not a coward, not scared of what one little kiss awakened in you."

"Think that kiss awoke somethin'?"

"I do."

He leaned down, until mere inches separated his mouth from hers. The weight of his arms about her middle felt so darn good, so right. It would be so easy to close the distance between them, to initiate another kiss. She fairly salivated at the thought of pressing her lips to his.

"I'm no coward," he whispered.

"Prove it."

He shook his head. "I think it was an anomaly. A freak thing. Random like a lightning strike. You'd just been through an ordeal, and it was gratitude and relief speaking."

But he hadn't pulled away. His words issued a challenge of their own—daring her to prove that kiss high in the mountain canyon, when she'd been nearly frozen and scared she'd spend a night in the forest in December.

"I was happy to see you."

"In that moment, you would've kissed anyone."

She raised one brow. "I might've kissed my brother on the cheek. But that kiss?" She leaned nearer, wondering if he sensed half the pull toward her that she did toward him. She'd never been so incredibly forward, but found she didn't, couldn't, regret it. "That was for you alone."

The light faded further, making it even harder to see his expression, the clarity of his eyes. Oh, but she wanted to.

He shrugged.

"You doubt me?"

"Prove it." His whispered plea was all the prompting she needed.

She touched her lips to his and found herself swept into a kiss as powerful as the first. Only this one had a sense of longing that was infinitely deeper.

This kiss promised a beginning.

"I love you." Emotion demanded she speak. "I love *you*, Gus."

She snuggled against the warm hollow of his throat, savoring the moment, the rush of affection vibrating in her soul.

He stilled.

He must feel the power of that kiss, the same miraculous bond.

Love between a man and a woman. *Precious. Healing. Permanent.*

Stillness led to a deep breath. His broad chest expanded and with hands upon her shoulders, set her back.

Cold wind stole between them, and in the near-dark, she glimpsed his hardened expression.

Euphoria shattered.

Her Gus was gone—only the stern lawman remained.

Rejection struck hard and fast, a surprise attack, not unlike the moment the Ruffians had grabbed her from the safety of the kitchen.

Oh, *why* had she opened her mouth?

Things had been perfect—

"Noelle." Gus's voice was as stern as his posture. "This isn't the time. I can't—"

White-hot pain gripped her heart, her chest—

How *dare* he? He couldn't know what she felt. He couldn't read her mind.

But she'd known, hadn't she? From the very beginning.

One stumbled step, then two. She flung open the screen door and pushed inside.

Heat and light. Family. Crowds.

Faces of loved ones turned to her, questions and concern on their faces.

She couldn't bear it.

She dashed up the stairs, her wool skirts in

her fists.

The slam of her bedroom door, and twist of the key in the lock weren't enough.

A brick wall one hundred feet high and a mile wide would never be enough.

Gus was in her heart to stay.

For a year, she'd loved a man who didn't want to love her in return.

She stifled a sob, refused to let anyone in this over-crowded house hear her cry.

An hour after Noelle stormed into the house, Gus *still* wanted to go to her. He dropped the stack of Ruffian portraits onto the desktop, pushed back the chair, and turned to glare at his crude map, tacked to the wall.

Every notation, X in blue pencil, and date chafed.

At least Noelle wasn't still barricaded in the bedroom she shared with two younger sisters. He'd heard her mother go to her, their soft voices directly overhead from his place in the ranch office room. At that moment, Noelle was in the kitchen with her mother, Deputy Murphy and Deputy Dillinger. The men had lingered after the town meeting.

Gus hadn't relied solely on the men's promises to keep an eye on Noelle. He'd crept down the hall and seen so for himself. Noelle worked with her mother, Effie, and Miranda to get supper on the table. Both Deputy Sheriffs sat at the table.

The curtains were closed against the darkness outside, just as he'd ordered. Good. If the gang was out there, they wouldn't track Noelle through the windows.

He blinked, aggravated by the constant preoccupation. The map couldn't hold his attention. He blinked, tried to refocus, and lost the fight.

He rubbed a palm over the ache in his chest.

I love you, Gus.

A distraction he couldn't afford. Not now. He intended to ride with the posse tomorrow, no matter what Phil Finlay wanted, and he couldn't actively pursue the gang and leave his brain box here, engrossed in kisses, and tangled up in Noelle.

He needed a clear head and all his wits. He needed to be sharp if he'd survive the coming confrontation with the Ruffians.

That's all it came down to.

He had no right to tie Noelle to him with talk of love. Not 'til he knew if he'd be around next week or next month. Maybe once the gang was safely in the State Penitentiary, the time would finally be right to confess love for Noelle.

He loved her. Probably had for a long while. The last few days had shown him that.

The girl was only nineteen.
They had time.
If he survived.

Noelle parted the kitchen curtain and glimpsed Gus through the frosted windowpanes, putting out his cigarette beneath his boot heel.

This isn't the time.

His rejection stung. Badly.

She'd wanted an *I love you too.*

Mother had followed her upstairs, listened, and reminded her that men stewed about one thing at a time. Gus's head was full of the Ruffian Gang. His thoughts should be on solutions. Tomorrow morning, he must direct the posse's search.

The town expected results. Gus bore that burden alone.

He leaned heavily on the railing, anxiety pressing upon his shoulders. He might think he'd hidden the worst of it from her, and initially he had. But mother's wisdom had opened her eyes.

Given the circumstances, she understood.

Flame lit his face as he cupped the Lucifer and another cigarette about his mouth. The deepening darkness made the flash of light all the brighter. Stark lines, sharp cheekbones—all the sharper for the pressure the town had put on him.

Though Noelle wanted to, she would not approach him now. He obviously needed to clear his head.

The stove lid clanged. Water sloshed in the wash basin. Footsteps thudded in the hallway toward the front of the house. Her heart might be broken, but she needed to help get supper on the table.

She let the curtain fall, and worked with her sisters to set both the kitchen and dining room tables.

The deputies sat at the kitchen table with Cliff, scheduling guard duty, worked out who would see to chores, and determined who would make a trip to town the following morning for supplies. Despite the posse, or maybe because of the posse and all the extra mouths to feed, Ma was in dire need of supplies.

The official deputies, Murphy and Dillinger, had included the official-but-young deputized Timothy and Dallas. Her little brothers took their work seriously. The boys pushed past her for their coats and headed outside, likely carrying a message to the bunkhouse.

Mother conversed with Deputy Dillinger in front of the dresser that held table linens.

"Pardon me, Ma." Once they'd stepped aside, Noelle opened the drawer for and brought out napkins.

She stood at the table, folded a napkin and slipped it beneath the fork at Ma's place. She moved on to the next, pausing to bask in contentment. Surrounded by friends and family, snug in the sanctuary of her home, made her savor the security all who loved her had rallied to provide.

"Miss Noelle?" Cliff waited at her elbow. "You feelin' all right?"

Not odd—at least not coming from Cliff. He'd been there...the other half of the team that had found her last night. She'd been so focused on Gus, she'd barely noticed the hired hand. Had she thanked him last night?

"Just tired. Thank you for asking. And thank you for your help last night. I'm grateful."

"You're welcome, Miss Noelle. Just doin' my job." He glanced at Mother and Deputy Dillinger, still deep in conversation.

"Given your ma's tied up at the moment, think you could get me the grocery list? I'm told I drew the short straw, and I'll take the wagon to town tomorrow morning for groceries."

"You'd rather ride?"

Cliff, loyal and steadfast, was a natural in the saddle and took charge of moving cattle from one range to another as seasons changed. She'd be surprised if he didn't prefer posse duty over errands.

"Yes, ma'am. But I like to eat too. I hear the flour barrel is empty and the pantry's low on sugar. I do like hot bread and sweet cake and can't have either without flour and sugar."

She chuckled. "I'll get the list."

If Gus had come in from the back porch, she'd not seen nor heard him. She knocked, listened, and when she heard no reply, opened the door a crack to find the office dark. Thank goodness Gus hadn't returned.

Rather than light the lamp, she left the door open wide. Light filtered in from other rooms.

Her drawings covered the old pine desk Pa had built when he'd still operated the carpentry shop. Gus had hung his map on the wall.

At disruption of indirect light spilling in from the hallway, she glanced back, surprised Cliff had followed her from the kitchen. His tall frame blocked much of the light, but she found the list, where Mother always kept it, beneath a glass paperweight on her own little writing desk.

"Much obliged, Miss Noelle."

Cliff's voice sounded directly behind her. Close. Too close.

The hired hand had seen her in Gus's arms. Surely he knew they'd begun an odd but genuine courtship. Did he think to declare himself, anyhow? Would it be necessary to tell him she had eyes only for Gus?

His hand, big and gruff, settled on her shoulder.

"Mr. Cox—"

He silenced her with a brutal hold over her mouth.

Betrayal sluiced through her.

She tasted blood.

Cliff Cox?

She'd been fooled—they'd *all* been fooled.

They'd trusted the wrong man.

Noelle's stomach dropped as Cliff Cox—the traitorous cowhand—locked an arm about her ribs, immobilizing her arms.

Her mind seized. Laughter in the front parlor continued, Papa's guffaws loudest among them. As she fought for air, Cliff's hot breath stirred hairs near her ear.

A scraping sound came from the window, wood chafing against wood. Someone inched up in the unlocked window sash.

Unlocked.

This time of year, especially *now,* with the extra care they'd taken, every window had remained locked.

A Judas had unlocked the ground-floor window, because a shadowed figure's hands eased up the window.

In one bright moment of startling clarity, she comprehended she'd been gone from the kitchen mere seconds, in the company of a trusted employee. Inside her own home. *Safe*—or so everyone believed.

For the *second time*, the gang snagged her from home and dragged her into the winter night.

She should fight, should make noise to alert the others, literally in the next room.

Cliff, so much stronger than she, bodily picked her up by the middle and walked her closer to the window.

Fight. Kick. Stomp!

She'd frozen, the commands to react in those

precious seconds whizzing past at blinding speed.

She couldn't force her legs, the only part of her free, to obey.

Panic erupted low in her belly, surged upward in a rush of heat, filled her chest, and clogged her throat. Her vision tunneled.

All that remained was the vice-like constriction of a seasoned cow-hand's unbreakable grip. *She couldn't breathe.*

Lights flashed in the dimness.

She'd suffocate.

Die.

Panic hurled her lower limbs into motion.

Woolen carpet muffled her boots. Against Cliff's size and strength, she was helpless.

He breathed ragged chuffs at her ear.

At the edge of the rug she seized her last chance, her flagging consciousness, and stomped hard against the floorboards. Her knee connected with the wall beneath the window frame.

Papa!

Blood surged against her ears, muting her hearing, but she knew her best efforts hadn't been good enough.

Gus!

The chance was lost.

Bitter, icy wind snaked through the open window, stealing her body heat.

The terror she'd battled in the canyon, in her nightdress, returned full-force.

Cliff hefted her off her feet and attempted to force her lower body through the window. His cohort grabbed for her boots.

She kicked wildly, fought for air.

With brutal force, Cliff wrenched her head one direction and her ribs the other, as if he'd snap her neck. Terror seized her heart, already galloping wildly against her corset.

"Come quietly now, Missy, or I'll shut you up, permanent-like. The Marshal won't know any different. Either way, we'll get him."

Cliff Cox *would* end her life.

Without reason, without regret.

If dead, she'd have no chance to thwart the gang's efforts to kill Gus.

She didn't want to die.

She valued her life...it had barely begun. She still had much to do, many things to accomplish.

Forcing a ruthless man to break her neck or silence her with a knife slid between her ribs would do her no good. Would do *Gus* no good.

She seized her *final* option and surrendered control of her body.

Let him think she'd swooned in terror. Or lost consciousness due to lack of air.

His arms, twisted chains, remained locked about her for several long seconds.

Though her eyelids had drifted shut, she sensed as much as felt a man grab her skirts and tug her nearer the window.

"Pass her through." He'd whispered, but she knew the rasp of his voice. Of all the crew, he'd made her the most uncomfortable. He'd have been first in line, had Boss given the go-ahead to attack.

Cliff's iron grip relaxed, just a little, testing.

She let her head loll to the side as he finally released his hold on her mouth.

They manhandled her. How many hands? How many men?

She risked opening her eyes to slits.

Shadows of men surrounded her. More than one or two had waited outside for Cliff to subdue her.

Outnumbered, out-muscled, and without a weapon, she couldn't save herself.

Not yet.

If she succeeded in convincing them she'd swooned, they might not drug her this time. She might recognize landmarks, might walk away from them again—if they believed she didn't know where she was.

More importantly, if she stayed alive, she'd have a chance to save Gus.

Screaming now would provoke the devils into knifing or shooting her immediately. The noise would alert Gus and her family.

He'd come after her in a blind rage.

Unprepared, careless, and incautious, he'd give the bandits what they wanted...a dead U.S. Marshal.

Gus ignored the bitter cold and savored his cigarette.

The tobacco calmed his nerves. As soon as he

finished his third, his frame of mind would be much improved.

He'd tackle the photographs again.

If he knew who the people were, or at least *Boss*, he'd infer the root of their vengeance. Knowing who they were would also narrow down hidey-holes significantly.

Which meant tomorrow's posse would succeed in the hunt.

They'd oust the varmints, and put an end to their terrorizing.

By so doing, he'd regain the respect of the community. They'd trust him again. He'd belong.

Which meant he'd be at peace. Comfortable.

Most importantly, he'd be able to ask Phil Finlay for permission to court his daughter in earnest.

He could make Noelle his bride and finally, *finally* start living.

Easy to see it now that so much existing was behind him. All those years wasted, waiting for Effie, wanting Effie.

Funny, wasn't it?

He'd spent the whole day in the same house as her, bumped into her a couple times, and hadn't been obsessed with her or all he'd lost. Not for a single minute.

Every distracting thought had been of Noelle.

He took one last drag on his cigarette, the thing burned so low it scorched his fingertips. He dropped it to the porch and ground it out. He blew out the smoke through his nose and with his face turned toward the first evening stars twinkling their faint light, allowed the parade of Noelle's portraits to flash through his mind.

This time, he animated the two-dimensional images as flesh-and-blood men. With heat to their skin and vibrant life in their eyes. He imagined movement in the set of their shoulders. Attitude. Personality. Lack of conscience.

One by one, from the bottom of the pecking order on up.

Maybe there was something familiar about the lead man, the one they called Boss. When Noelle had taken her artist pencils to that drawing after breakfast, bringing the image to life in shades of blond and brown, a bit of green and blue in the brown of his eyes a whisper of memory had tugged, itched, and played hide-and-go-seek.

He turned back to Boss in his mind's eye, animated him again.

Inside the house, he heard all the usual sounds...laughter among the men in the parlor, the clank of a lid on the stove as Mrs. Finlay put more fuel on the fire. The crisp knock of knuckles to a shut door somewhere upstairs. The clippity-clop of one of the young men clattering down the stairs full-speed.

"Noelle?" Mrs. Finlay's voice. Even and inquisitive.

Gus turned to the house, one last scan of the sheltering trees around the low bowl the Finlay house rested in. Wind danced in the evergreen boughs, standing as sentinels at the edge of the yard.

Light spilled from nearly every window in the big house. As far as the eye could see, nothing but the normal activity around the barn and bunkhouse, and clear, wide-open sky.

"Noelle?" Mrs. Finlay again, louder, panic coloring her tone.

Eleven

Gus yanked open the kitchen door.

He found Noelle's mother in the back hallway, headed to the front of the house as fast as she could go.

He caught her by the elbow. "Where is she?"

"I don't know. She was right there, in the kitchen with me—then she wasn't."

Gus pushed past her, into the parlor, took in the scattering of male bodies, lazing about on the sofas, sitting opposite one another at the chess board, Dallas napping on the rug before the fire. Blank expressions rapidly changed to incredulity.

"Noelle?" he bellowed.

Luke was the first on his feet. "She was in the kitchen with Ma. And both deputies."

"Cliff, too." Her father pushed to his feet, his age showing in the jerky movements.

But Cliff and the deputies weren't in the kitchen. Gus checked—*again*.

Where had they gone? If they'd headed out the kitchen door to the barn, he'd have seen them. That left the front door. "Anyone go out the front?"

"No." Phil scraped a shaking hand over his face. Caroline hid her face on her husband's chest. He held her tight.

The brothers spoke all at once.

"Nope."

"Didn't see nothin'."

"She gone?"

Gus wheeled about, fear a cold fist clamped on his throat. His heart chugged hard, a runaway locomotive down a steep grade. *How* had this happened? *How* had he lost her?

Stupid, *stupid*!

He'd laid eyes on her, what, half an hour past? If he'd stayed with her, kept her in the same room, put her to work doing something, *anything*, she'd be with him still.

No—if he'd told her he loved her. Pain tore through his gut, pounded through his skull. If he'd confessed his love for her, she might have been sitting in the parlor with him, secure and happy, her hand in his.

Love surged, mingled with panic, tied up tight and inseparable.

He took the stairs three at a time, burst into each and every bedroom, slamming the doors against opposite walls. "Noelle!"

Babies awoke and wailed. Downstairs, Caroline sobbed. Dallas and Timothy conducted an identical search on the main floor.

Gus's stomach heaved. If he'd eaten supper, he would've lost it right there, on Mrs. Finlay's clean upstairs hallway.

He'd failed the only person who mattered. Love and agony blended into a froth in his chest.

He'd failed the only test that had consequence.

Stupid, stupid, *stupid*!

His mind flashed from an image of Cliff to Elias and Raymond—his deputies. He'd left the men in the kitchen with Noelle and her mother. Were the three men working together?

"Look for her—*now*," he yelled at the startled sisters as he clomped back down the stairs. "Stay inside, but *find her*."

He bounded down the stairs, shoved past a knot of young men, searching faces for those who'd seen her last. "Raymond. Elias. Cliff. *Where are they*?"

"Here, Sheriff." Both deputies, right behind the knot of brothers. "We were in the dining room, working out a trade for guard shift."

"That doesn't matter—not anymore." God help him, nothing mattered anymore. He had to get to Noelle, *now*.

She wouldn't have headed to the necessary. She'd been cooperative. Stayed in the presence of several family members. For Pete's sake, he'd seen her peeking at him from behind the kitchen curtains not ten minutes earlier.

His heart pounded. "Where's Cliff?"

"Don't know." Murphy looked to Dillinger.

"He didn't come out back." Three cigarettes. No one had gone through that door but himself.

The men who'd lounged in the front parlor shook their heads. No Cliff.

Noelle's sisters clattered down the stairs.

"He was in this house—" Gus's throat closed.

"She's not up there," one sister cried. "We searched. Everywhere."

Cliff Cox...

Heaven help them all.

One way or the other, Cliff had gone missing with Noelle. He might have been subdued and carried off against his will. Or he might be a bad egg.

Gus leaned toward the bad egg theory. 'Cause somebody on the inside had to have unlocked a window. No other egress made sense.

"Sheriff?" Phil demanded, in the broken tones of a grieving parent.

Gus's stomach pitched. Finally, the pieces of this puzzle slid into place with a nearly audible click.

"Cliff Cox has her." A lackey. Persuaded by money, most likely. If it turned out Cox was innocent, Gus would apologize. The man was guilty 'til proved innocent.

He banged through the office door, grabbed her stack of lifelike images, his hands shaking. His heart tripped over itself, rolled, and slammed against his ribs. He riffled through the pencil drawings, tossing the top two, then three.

Luke struck a match, lit the lamp. Hot light spilled over the face of the man they called Boss.

There.

Boss was none other than Jedediah Smythe, Esquire. Dark brown hair cut short, fully shaved, expensive suit of clothes. The posture of a confident and successful attorney, grilling Gus on the witness stand.

He saw it now, beneath the reddish beard, the sun-bleached, unkempt hair so long it brushed his shoulders. Beneath the tanned skin lurked the attorney who'd blamed Gus.

Gus's testimony had led to the conviction of Zachary Evans, Jedediah Smythe's half-brother, for the murder of Judge Rathburn. He'd died less than a week later, knifed in an inmate brawl.

The last puzzle piece lay figuratively in his hand.

Boss wanted a life for a life.

He'd held onto the hope that they wanted *his* life, not Noelle's. Yes, Jedediah wanted Gus to suffer as he'd suffered the loss of his brother.

If he'd pegged the warped motivation, the gang would wait to kill her until Gus arrived, to make him undergo the horror as they took her life.

They wanted Gus to follow—and that might be their Achilles Heel.

He grabbed his coat, bellowed for the others to follow, and bolted for the barn and their mounts.

With a half-pint of luck, they had a chance of overtaking the gang, freeing Noelle, and capturing at least part of the vermin.

If they so much as broke the delicate skin at her wrists with rope, he'd see them shot through the heart.

No citified trial for them.

They'd caught themselves a spitting-mad U.S. Marshal.

Watch out, boys. Here I come.

The men had gagged her, tied her wrists and ankles, tossed her over a saddle, and left her to jostle and bounce with every running step the mare took on its lead rope. She'd given up any pretense of unconsciousness and did her best to hold on. A thick knot secured her bonds to the front cinch strap.

She'd escaped once. They wouldn't trust her again.

Five horses, maybe six, bolted once they'd reached the main road.

The threat of a brutal death, dragged beneath running hooves, stole her sanity. Numb from the bitter cold and the ropes biting into her flesh, her hold slipped. She jounced on the saddle, her ribs bruising. Blood pounded in her head. She fought for a secure hold on the cinch strap and finally managed.

Winter sliced through her gray woolen dress,

her petticoats and stockings. She shivered uncontrollably from fear and below-freezing temperatures.

Despite her confession of love, he would come for her again.

That eventuality terrified her more than the risk of being trampled.

He'd lead a speedy charge to her rescue. Most of the riders would be her immediate family. Pa. Luke. Gerald. Timothy and Dallas. Hunter, Miranda's husband. They'd follow swiftly...if they could discern their fresh tracks from those left by the many visitors earlier in the day.

After what seemed to be an hour, but it couldn't have been so long, the party left the road and swung about sharply.

Behind an outcropping of rock, more men waited with lanterns.

In an instant, she identified the location. Dead Man's Drop—a narrow pass between the mountainside and an enormous boulder that had crashed to the earth long before white men settled Colorado.

Coming from the ranch, Gus would never see the Ruffian Gang until it was too late, 'til her family had ridden through the narrow neck of road between the boulder and mountainside. They'd be on the lookout for the gang ahead.

The Ruffian Gang intended an ambush—*right here*. They'd slaughter her family.

Bile burned her throat. Her empty stomach, abused by the saddle and unnatural motion, churned with nausea. If she vomited into her gag, she'd suffocate. With her wrists tied, she might wrench the cloth free from her mouth, but at great risk to her precarious balance across the saddle.

She fought to clear her pounding head by breathing deeply through her nose, forcing her respirations to slow.

With her head still lower than her heart, her ears pounded in time with her racing pulse. She must *do* something, beginning with freeing herself.

A rhythmic thumping of a mallet rang against wood. Were they driving a stake into the frozen earth?

She darted a glance both left and right. No one watched her.

Before she could think too hard, she wiggled, pulled, and kicked her bound feet. Gravity worked in her favor. She tumbled, landing on her rump in the snow. The incredible pressure in her head immediately waned. The mare swung her head around and nickered at the unladylike dismount.

Noelle hadn't much time. Mother and Gus had kept a constant eye on her. They'd notice her missing within minutes.

Pulling on the cinch strap, fighting the lack of balance from trussed ankles, she finally made it to her feet. Yes! At this angle, it was possible to get a thumb beneath her gag and rip it—

"You gonna make me babysit you?" Slim, the outlaw who'd been kind, the first time around. Now sour-natured, narrow-eyed, and dangerous.

She froze, the gag barely out of her mouth.

"I'm—"

"Put that back." He pulled her hands away and shoved the wad of soggy fabric deep behind her teeth.

Fear collided with frustration and her stomach roiled. Not like it had when she'd been rump-high, but almost. She gagged.

Slim's eyes widened. He pointed a bony finger at her. "Now none of that."

She shook her head, desperate to convince him she *would* lose her stomach. Maybe the threat would be enough for him to skedaddle and leave her be long enough to wrest herself free of the restraints.

She squeezed her eyes shut in case he could see her lie in her eyes, and emphasized a dry heave. Playacting of course, but in her desperation, it was almost real.

"Aw, Jerusalem crickets!"

The gag muffled her moan, so she grumbled louder. The gurgle sounded an awful lot like she would, indeed, spew the gag down the front of Slim's jacket. He took a giant step away from her. He glanced over his shoulder at the rest of his gang.

From here, all movement had stopped with the gang settled in to wait. Lamps doused. With only a hint of moonlight peeking through the clouds, they seemed ready to pounce.

She strained to hear sounds of an approaching rescue party.

Not yet. Please, not yet.

If she didn't do something, and fast, this would end badly.

Her father, brothers, the man she loved—would be massacred.

Her stomach seized, and she barely had time to thrust her head close to her bound hands and wrench the gag free before she threw up.

"Come on, come on!" Gus swung into the saddle, wheeled Beau toward the gate, and gestured with the swing of an arm to the posse. If they hadn't managed to saddle up as fast as him, they'd have to ride hard and catch up.

Every second lost could cost Noelle her life.

The moon peeked from behind the nighttime clouds, illuminating the yard about the house just enough...disturbed snow drifts beneath the window on this side of the house. The office.

He'd made a circuit of the house just before those three cigarettes, and not a single footprint had marred the pristine drifts of snow.

The churned mass revealed many more footprints less than fifteen feet from that window—the way they'd obviously stolen Noelle.

He held up a hand to silence the others. He glanced, quick enough to see nearly all the men had caught up. He stood in the stirrups and tried to untangle the tell-tale signs on the bare canvas of the side yard where they meshed with the drive toward the gate.

If the whole yard hadn't been trampled by that impromptu town meeting, he'd be able to see precisely what had happened.

Almost as if her captors had taken the time to arrange two dozen pebbles into the shape of an arrow, pointing the way, he discerned where they'd cut across the yard, snaking their way around the front—unseen by everyone behind the lacy curtains at the parlor windows—and headed due west.

As expected, they *wanted* him to follow. The gang had to guess he'd be less than five minutes behind.

He scanned the countryside and strained to listen. Nothing.

"Which way, Sheriff?" Phil's warm breath clouded his face. Hiding his identity.

In that instant, Gus knew what the gang would do, If not precisely where.

"Where would you go, less than two miles from here, to set up an ambush?"

The Finlay men glanced at each other.

Luke shifted in the saddle. "Dead Man's Drop."

Gus knew the place, but not well.

"Ambush?" Dallas's voice sounded small. Like a child.

"Maybe you ought to stay home, son." Phil gestured toward the house. "Watch out for your mama."

"I'm a Deputy Sheriff, Pa. I have responsibilities."

"Other options?" Gus demanded. If Dead

Man's Drop wasn't the place...

"That's it." Phil nodded with certainty. "Fits the bill perfectly. Only place like it within twenty miles."

With a sweep of his arm, Gus touched his heels to Beau's flanks and set out at a run, the others following.

Noelle bent at the waist, breathed through her mouth, and fought ongoing nausea. She spat, trying to clear her mouth.

"Did ya have to go and do that?" Slim's loud whisper barely carried to her ears. He avoided the sour mess, giving it a wide berth, grabbed her elbow and jerked her upright.

And to think this man had been solicitous during her captivity in the cabin.

Something had definitely changed.

Without warning, Slim and two other men wrestled her into submission. One wrenched her arms behind her back while another pulled her teeth apart and shoved the gag back in.

Panic had her fighting, kicking, attempting the impossible—to free herself from three much stronger men.

Boss, who'd not been paying her a lick of attention until now, stepped into her line of sight. Two long strides, and he pointed a blunt forefinger in her face. "I don't much care if you're dead or alive when the illustrious August Rose comes for you, woman."

Something hard and pointed jabbed her ribs. A pistol?

Terror snaked its way up her spine, rendering her motionless in the overpowering grip of her enemies.

Boss's breath fanned her face, warm and surprisingly fresh with a recent brushing.

The ridiculous idea that he'd focus on oral hygiene in preparation for tonight's outing made her incredulous. But the jab of a pistol barrel—she would bruise, if she lived long enough to care—demanded her attention.

"Do I," Boss said softly, almost like a courtly gentleman, "make myself clear?"

She nodded, jerking. Her stomach heaved.

She would *not* vomit behind the gag. She couldn't.

Boss dismissed her, turning to his minions. "Get her on the nag."

It was too dark to see who led a dark horse forward, but the toss of the animal's head and the way its ears pricked and twitched had a bad omen. She twisted against the bonds securing her wrists behind her back. She'd have a hard time staying in the saddle, even with the full use of her hands upon the reins and soothing the beast with crooning sounds.

She had no choice.

The men hefted her onto the saddle. "Swing a leg over, Missy." He hiked up her skirts. Someone else grabbed her calf and pulled her leg over the horse's back. If she weren't furious, she'd be embarrassed.

Freezing air stung through her wool stockings. Her toes had numbed with cold, and that made finding the stirrups, set far too long for her legs, impossible. The horse flinched and Noelle hung on with her knees. Terror clogged her throat and made it impossible to draw enough breath through her nose.

She would die.

Tonight.

Whether thrown from this horse or by the hand of one of her captors.

Brilliant light flared as someone put a match to a torch and the fuel caught.

Her mount pinned its ears, shuffled two or three steps to the rear, and finally responded to the tug on its halter to move forward.

Through the narrow pass, toward home.

Where Gus would see her by the light of that burning torch when he rounded the bend.

Rough hands shoved a loop of rope over her head. Specks of light flashed before her eyes. She fought for air, couldn't breathe!

A noose.

What a *waste*. She'd only had nineteen short years. Hadn't even seen her nineteenth birthday, likely never would. She'd had too few days with Gus. A handful of kisses.

It wasn't enough.

Twelve

The moon slipped behind a gauzy veil of clouds, shading the snowy landscape an inky blue.

The well-traveled road had turned to slushy mud, churned under countless hooves, wagon wheels and sleighs, slowing the rescue party's progress.

In his gut, he *knew* Jedediah Smythe intended to end this. Tonight.

That meant ensuring Gus followed.

Jed had obviously started on this road. If he deviated from it, he'd make obvious tracks.

Elevation climbed as the road veered around a curve to the right. What began as a gentle slope from the shoulder of the road gradually became a sheer cliff for fifty yards, he recalled, and around another sharp bend came the landmark the locals referred to as Dead Man's Drop.

The image of Smythe's calculated smile that day in the courtroom paraded through Gus's memory. He pulled Beau up short.

Smythe had the sharpest mind Gus had encountered. In the Service or since.

And he'd had *months* to plan.

Only a fool would ride in, heedless, endangering his own life and the lives of Noelle's loved ones.

Or expect the set-up to be simple.

Gus swallowed a litany of curses.

With Jed Smythe, *nothing* would be simple.

He held up a hand to silence the men. Horses blew puffs of white. Beneath him, Beau side-stepped and tossed his head. The gelding sensed the threat.

At any moment, the entire gang might open fire from the dense evergreens on both sides of the road. Why hadn't he seen that threat before he'd lined his men up like sitting ducks?

As if circling a lariat, he motioned for the group to turn about, and led the retreat. They halted at the main intersection where sparse foliage provided poor cover.

"We'll divide up, approach from three sides." The steep mountainside shielded the fourth. "Phil, I want you and the boys to skirt around, come at them from the far side. Stay back 'til the shooting starts. Don't let 'em retreat."

He turned to Noelle's elder brothers. "They're

expecting us to charge through, in pursuit. I need at least six of us so it looks and sounds like our whole party. Ride tight with me to the gate. I'll charge through while you wheel about and fire on anything that moves."

Murphy shook his head with vehemence. "Sheriff, you can't—"

"Don't hand yourself over." Luke yelled over the top of Murphy. "Noelle will tan my hide for shoe leather if I don't stop you."

Twin Colts provided reassuring weight in his holsters. "I'll charge into the hornet's nest, and I'll fight. With all of 'em focused on me," —*he prayed*— "I'm counting on you three to get Noelle out."

Noelle.

Everything came down to her. *Nothing* else mattered. Not Gus's reputation with the people of Mountain Home. Not proving himself worthy to the naysayers. Nor to Luke and Effie Finlay. In fact, it seemed like years since those factors mattered.

"Hunter, I need your gun arm."

Hunter nodded in consent.

"As we approach, you hold back. Watch for them to pop up like Prairie Dogs. Shoot to kill. If it moves, and it ain't wearing a skirt, kill it."

Hunter sat taller. "Yes sir."

"Dollars to donuts, they've got one or more men layin' low on the boulder, ready to take a shot at us riding in. I figure they don't much care when they put a bullet between my eyes, nor who else they shoot in the mayhem."

Gerald cursed. "We're dead men."

Phil hooked a thumb over his shoulder. "Go home, son. No one's forcing you to risk your life."

"I might do that."

Gerald's wife and children waited back at the house. Chances were he'd never been in a gunfight. "If the wind doesn't blow in our favor, the women and children will need protection—you can do that. Go on. No hard feelings."

The older man shifted, uncomfortable and indecisive.

Gus couldn't wait. He spoke to the rest of the posse. "It's *me* Smythe wants. Noelle's survival—" He choked on a heart so full it bobbed in his throat. *How* had he believed himself incapable of loving Noelle? Why had he clung to that mistaken identity, and allowed it to ruin his happiness *and* hers?

He'd wasted so much time and a wealth of opportunities. *Stupid.*

He held her father's eye. "I love Noelle." Agonized, he regretted not telling her himself. The words came easily. He could have. *Should* have. "She's worth *any* price. You tell her that. For me."

Phil nodded, and didn't make a condescending remark about Gus telling her himself. They both knew he wouldn't survive.

Gus recovered himself. "Deputies Murphy and Dillinger, take up firing positions on the downhill side." No sense getting both green deputies killed if he could prevent it. Somebody needed to survive and see remaining Ruffians transported to Cañon City.

"Ready to ride?" Gus asked.

The space of two heartbeats passed.

"You think she's still alive?" Luke asked.

"I know it. They need her for a bargaining chip. If this goes South, and this conflict doesn't end tonight, they'll need leverage."

Gus held Luke's gaze then looked to Phil, the deputies, the rest of Noelle's brothers. They'd all stand as witnesses. Someone would ensure she knew how much Gus had loved her. He locked on Gerald. "I meant what I said. I'll ride into the fires of hell to reclaim her."

Gus expected trouble.

If only he could double-guess Jed Smythe…

As agreed, Gus led the posse hard and fast toward Dead Man's Drop, praying the others were already in position. He strained to hear any indication of movement over the thunder of four horses' hooves, but detected nothing.

Until they rounded the bend, and the site came into view.

He'd expected full dark, men hiding beyond the fallen granite boulder, not a sign of the bandits.

Until they'd plowed through the narrow pass to the other side and every expectation sizzled and disappeared, water drops on a hot skillet.

Jumpin' Jehoshaphat.

Torchbearers, one on each side of the narrow

pass, shed more than enough light on the roadway for Gus to realize several vital details all at once.

A single rider sat on a nervous horse, right in the middle of that pass. That rider was a woman—*Noelle.*

The miscreants had bound her hands behind her back and strung a noose around her neck. The rope looped up and over downed telegraph pole.

They intended to *hang* Noelle?

Here. *Now.*

Gus pulled back on the reins, halting Beau. Noelle's brothers slowed and stopped. They waited four abreast, then five as Gerald caught up, across the road.

Her eyes rounded, and if it weren't for the gag in her mouth, she'd have yelled. Torchlight caught on tears streaming down her cheeks.

Love and compassion for his woman were instantly elbowed aside by rougher, angrier emotions. Fury and shock warred for dominance. Both prevented him from solving the conundrum. He was supposed to trade his life for hers.

Jedediah Smythe wanted Gus's hide?

He could have it—as long as Noelle went free.

Behind him, he heard the unmistakable clatter of Hunter levering a bullet into the chamber.

If only he could see beyond that broad circle of light, get a better glimpse of where the men were, how many guns were aimed at their hearts.

Noelle's frantic movement, shaking her head side to side in an obvious communication of *no!,* caught his attention and wouldn't release him.

How could he ensure her safety? His heart galloped rapidly in his chest, and the world around him slowed, stretched like warm molasses taffy...

And he simply knew what he had to do. With his pistol in hand, it took a mere second to draw a bead on the unlucky bastard holding the far end of the hangman's noose. Dead, he couldn't hold the rope, and if his shot startled the horse beneath Noelle, she wouldn't hang.

They'd expected this, of course, for in the same long second, the guy holding the torch swung it in a long arc backward, shedding revealing light on Gus's target—Noelle's *father* held that rope, at gunpoint.

In his gut, he knew Phil would rather drop the rope and take a close-range bullet than be party to his daughter's hanging. But Jed wouldn't have left anything like this to chance. There would be more men aiming at Phil, others prepared to take his place, to secure the rope.

If only he could see!

Gus spun his wrist, pointed his Colt at the heavens, and disengaged the hammer.

Beau tossed his head, sidestepped, and Gus's mind whirled. With sharp clarity, every sense on highest alert, he took note of Luke, Hunter, and Gerald, rifles aimed, their mounts moved into place flanking him on both sides.

The odds had changed, and not in their favor. If Phil had been captured, then chances were, so had Timothy and Dallas. That meant no one watched the gang's backs. With those three out of commission, their odds were terrible. He'd be lucky if a single Finlay came out of this altercation alive.

It wasn't supposed to have gone down like this.

Gus made a show of tossing both beloved Colts into the muddy road. Moving slowly, as to not disturb the high-strung horse beneath Noelle, he dismounted. "Jedediah Smythe!"

Silence. Saddle leather creaked. Gus's heart raced, pounding in his ears, but he fancied he heard Noelle's muffled cries behind her gag.

Despite the silence, he knew he'd identified the correct man. Smythe no doubt toyed with him, refusing to answer, making him question himself.

He met her gaze, tried his best to communicate his love for her, his reasons—only one, really—for putting an end to this. The only end that had a sliver of a chance of seeing her alive at sunrise. He prayed she'd not be witness to the murders of her father, brothers, and friends.

Long seconds passed.

The horse beneath Noelle shuffled, nervous, its reins trailing in the mud.

Gus put up both hands, took two slow, easy steps closer to his death. The whole time, he held Noelle's gaze with his.

This woman held his heart. His worn out, hand-me-down, tattered heart had settled so fully on her, he had zero choice.

He had to try and win her safety by sacrificing

himself to Jed's gang.

He had no confidence the man would take him in her stead, and ultimately set her free. But one thing was clear. If Gus did nothing, she'd be lost forever. If not twisting and suffocating at the end of a poorly knotted noose, then by gunshot or worse.

He would not let that happen.

"Jed!" Gus held his breath, his gaze soaking up every detail of Noelle's beautiful eyes, the love brimming in her tears. "It's me you want. Take me, instead."

He swallowed hard, fought down the wobble that crept into his voice. "Let her go."

Thirteen

Noelle's heart shuddered and threatened to stop completely. Had she ever been this furious at anyone? Were *all* men so dense?

Gus held her gaze, the torch light illuminating his dear face, as he walked into hell to save her.

What *was* he thinking?

It wouldn't work—she figured he knew that much.

He'd obviously figured out a thing or two, because he'd called one of the gang members by name—Jedediah Smythe. The name meant nothing to her, but it evidently meant a great deal to Gus. A man from his past. A man who knew him as U.S. Marshal Rose.

She would die, and because he hadn't the sense of a goose, he didn't know when to cut his losses and run away.

Thus, her death had no possibility of *meaning* anything.

If she could save him, she'd do it.

Gus deserved to *live*.

Tears of anger—fury at her captors, frustration with Gus, love for this heroic, wonderful man swelling in her to the point she couldn't hold the tears in any longer—ran down her cold cheeks in warm tracks.

Her nose started to stuff up. With a gag shoved in her mouth and her hands bound behind her back, she panicked. Drawing enough air suddenly became a much bigger problem.

She wanted to live.

The twitchy horse didn't like Gus's approach. It bobbed its head, pinned its ears, and nickered a warning. The rope about her neck drew taut, scraped across her throat, and pulled her posture straight. She squeezed the horse between her knees and held on.

Gus took another stride forward, his hands still up in that universal sign of surrender. Then another.

"Good of you to join us, Marshal." Boss's voice. Coming from the safety of the darkness beyond the pass.

"Just responding to your invitation, Jed." Gus's voice carried on the still air. He projected so all could hear.

Did he really intend to give himself up?

Her gaze darted back to where Luke, Gerald, and Hunter waited on their mounts, nearly beyond the reach of torchlight. Her heart pounded with growing anxiety—her brothers and brother-in-law needed to leave. They couldn't save her. They had families to live for.

Gus took her horse's bridle in his big, solid hand and steadied the beast, even as he spoke. "What do you say you come on out so we can make an exchange. Me for the girl."

Her heart rolled all the way over. Love for him had her shouting *no!* before she remembered the gag. The muffled, unintelligible sound brought Gus's attention back to her. Something in his luminous, storms-a-brewin' eyes begged her to trust him.

Trust? *Trust?*

Sit here and do *nothing* while he gave himself up to certain and horrendous death? Not if she could do anything about it.

A hint of a smile, so sad, so filled with an emotion she'd seen lingering in his eyes, touched Gus's mouth. *I love you.* He formed each word softly, carefully, as if he'd prefer no one else read his lips.

Love.

He loved her.

Now the idiot man realized what she'd known all along! Of course he loved her!

He formed the words silently, but so slowly she had no difficulty understanding exactly what he communicated.

His reason, then.

His justification for forfeiting the life she valued more than her own. How was she supposed to live with that knowledge? Whether she lived two minutes or two years or one hundred years longer than him, how could she survive, knowing he'd saved her with the only currency the Ruffian Gang would accept? The price of his life.

Noelle shook her head, vehemently determined to communicate. *No, oh, no you don't. You will* live, *August Rose. You'll live and that's final.*

He did smile then, a secret smile just for her. *Yes,* his mouth formed the words he did not speak aloud. *I love you.*

Noelle groaned. *Now* he decided to admit such an important truth she'd known for days. Longer, maybe. Right when she needed him to understand her wishes. She couldn't deny he loved her—*he loved her!*—but she also couldn't let him walk to his death without trying to stop him.

There had to be another way.

But he'd already turned away from her, his grip on the horse's halter still firm and walked the beast backward. The pressure on the rope stretching her neck eased.

...still doing everything he could to protect her.

She cast her attention over her shoulder, to see what the commotion was. How many men came through the narrow pass and into the light?

Were guns drawn? Would she witness Gus's death by shooting before she took a bullet in the back?

She couldn't turn far enough to see the action at her back, so she focused all of her attention on Gus. With his right hand holding the fidgeting horse's bridle, and his left in the air, he seemed relaxed, at ease, as if he faced down life-or-death situations every single day.

Maybe in New England, but not here. Not in calm, peaceable, law-abiding Mountain Home, where nothing like armed confrontations happened.

Still, his calm seeped into her. His silent cue for her to trust him washed through her again.

What plan did he have cooking?

But as seconds ticked past and no one approached Gus, she had the sinking realization that Boss would've sent his men to subdue Gus. Tie him up, confiscate any remaining weapons.

Wouldn't he?

If he intended to kill Gus, wouldn't he have by now? Why not simply aim and fire?

The waiting heightened her panic and had her blood surging in her ears at such a frantic pace she apparently hadn't heard a man approach until he spoke.

"We meet again." Boss's smooth voice. But yet it wasn't the gruff edge she'd typically heard. All that faded away and revealed the polish and culture beneath.

Noelle startled, turned to take in Boss's position, his *empty* hands. What, no gun?

She imagined every gang member at her back, their rifles targeting Gus's chest and her back.

Gus slowly lowered his free hand and as if in thoughtless, casual abandon, stroked the horse's muzzle in a soothing way she'd seen him do plenty of times with Beau.

Boss—Jed—didn't seem to notice, much less object.

"The honorable Jedediah Smythe, Esquire."

From the corner of her eye, she saw Boss bow, just a little, in recognition, with all the formality of a business meeting in a fine office in a big city. Not in the dark on a lonely road in the mountains of Colorado.

"I see you recall *why* your life holds the relative value of a Confederate penny."

His voice may have remained level, but venom had slipped into the statement, and Noelle feared Gus would react. Heavens, she *wanted* him to fight.

"I do recall. Your brother, Zachary Evans."

"His blood is on your hands, just as this young woman's will be."

Noelle's eyes filled with tears. Not because this whole mess had something to do with Gus's past, his time as a U.S. Marshal, but because Gus's honorable nature would burden him with guilt he didn't deserve. Gus had turned himself over to his enemy, without a shadow of hope to save her. Boss just as good as said her death was coming.

"A trade only seems just. I give myself up, unarmed and without resistance, and you let her walk away with her family."

"No, I don't think so." Jedediah—Boss—paused. "Very interesting, what you consider to be just. You showed no modicum of justice in the courtroom. You showed no measure of justice for my brother."

Was this true? It couldn't be. She'd had a full year of watching nearly everything August Rose did. And if anything, the man was just to a fault. He'd no doubt been doing his job as a Marshal when Boss's brother had his day in court. It obviously hadn't ended the way Boss wanted it to.

"Justice demands only the guilty are punished." Gus's voice iced over. "This woman is innocent. She had nothing to do with the proceedings in that courtroom, nor in the jail."

In the periphery of her vision, she saw Boss lift a shoulder in a negligent shrug. "An eye for an eye."

"That's not justice."

"You took someone I loved from me, Marshal, and now," Jed said, as calmly as if discussing the weather on a Sunday stroll in the park, "I take someone you love from you."

Noelle didn't need eyes in the back of her head to know what Jed had done. He'd stepped back a pace or so, out of her peripheral vision, but the expression on Gus's face, the tightness in his jaw and the set of his shoulders, the fierce clamp of his hands on the bridle of the horse told her everything she didn't want to know.

Jed had drawn his weapon, and most likely,

had it pointed at her back.

The breath seemed to jar in her lungs. She fell still, so still she may have been stone.

"Once that bit of comeuppance has been dispensed," Jed continued, "you will experience exactly what my brother did: a brawl with four larger, stronger men, to conclude with a shiv between your ribs. You will bleed into the mud at my feet. I will watch you die, slowly."

Jed's threats against Gus, the hold he had over their very lives, brought her back to herself. She flinched. She might be at their mercy, a noose about her neck and her hands tied securely behind her back, but her feet were free.

She knew that unseating herself from this animal would mean a slow, excruciating death. If she thought it difficult to breathe with a gag in her mouth, she'd soon know what it meant to dance at the end of a rope with her feet unable to find purchase.

Maybe the distraction would prove adequate to allow her brothers to fire. Or Gus would have the chance to attack.

If she jumped hard enough, she might have enough force to connect one of her remaining weapons—her feet—against her captor.

The thought of striking back, kicking the man with all the bottled-up fury and anger she felt made the unknown future worth it.

It seemed far better to die fighting than die a coward, his bullet in her back.

Gus clamped tighter on the horse's bridle. The animal wouldn't much like what would happen next, and with Phil Finlay holding the other end of his daughter's hanging rope—at gunpoint—this couldn't end well if the twitchy animal bolted.

His gaze remained locked with Jed's. Insanity flickered there. With the torches at Jed's back, his overgrown, sun-bleached hair glowed red like the fires of Hades.

With a practiced, swift move, Gus retrieved the derringer from his braces holster. So smoothly, so easily, he doubted Jed's men noticed.

Noelle shifted in the saddle, twisted as if she intended to throw her leg over the horse's neck and sit sidesaddle—

He risked pulling his attention away from Jed long enough to glare at her—just as she did exactly as he feared. What was the woman thinking?

He'd best let her in on his plan, now, before she did something stupid and got them both killed.

Done hiding his weapon, Gus clicked the hammer back. The audible sound couldn't have reached the men hiding in the darkness beyond the fallen boulder and through the pass. But Jed's gaze fastened on the tiny pistol.

"Call your men off." Gus kept his voice deliberately low. Only Jed and Noelle would have heard him.

In his periphery, Noelle stiffened as she sat awkwardly sidesaddle and, thank goodness, held still.

His attention remained focused on Jed who simply drew a lazy smile, tipped his head back and chuckled.

"Do it." Gus eased a bit closer. At less than twelve inches, a shot to the chest would spell the end for Jedediah. Laughter seemed the most irrational response.

"Now, Marshal, what you don't seem to comprehend is you're outgunned. Outnumbered." He glanced back over his shoulder, and the red of his beard caught the firelight turning it brilliant. "No one believed you'd walk in here, unarmed. We took...precautions."

Gus's heart tripped sideways. He knew they had a rifle trained on Noelle's father...but he had the most unwelcome suspicion they'd taken the upper hand in more ways than that. "As did I."

"That so?" Jed clucked, as if verbal sparring was his primary goal. "Shame, shame." He clucked his tongue. "You sent five good men to their deaths. Rather a nasty habit of yours."

Five: Phil, Timothy, Dallas, Deputies Dillinger and Murphy. Was it possible even one of them had evaded the outlaws' notice?

"Five seconds," Gus countered. "Call them off, or I shoot to kill."

Jed held Gus's gaze, without a glimmer of fear or doubt.

"Four." Gus swallowed. He hated this sensation of running into a dark alley, outgunned, without a chance in a million of coming out alive.

He'd done that. Once. And lived to tell the tale. "Three."

"You assume I wish to live, Marshal. That would be your first mistake."

"Evidently you wish to live long enough to slip a shiv between my ribs, as you said. You can't watch me bleed out if you're dead."

Push had come to shove. Without concern who in the shadows might see his weapon or his intent to strike, Gus took aim. The time for discussion was over. He'd put one bullet neatly through Jed's heart and end this standoff. He gripped the nervous horse's bridle ever tighter. No way would he sacrifice Noelle's life this close to—

Light caught on a flash of metal, an arc sweeping toward his ribs, his unprotected side beneath his gun arm.

He took a hit in the ribs, blunt force that felt far more like a left-hook than the slash of a blade, even through the thick layers of his coat, two shirts, and union suit.

He danced back, a reflex, just as a flash of petticoats blocked his view. He would have fired, but somehow, Noelle had put herself between him and his target.

The fool horse backed up, whipped its head, attempting to evade Gus's grip. Noelle leaped from the saddle and Gus's heart nearly exploded.

Gunfire erupted. From behind him, on the mountainside, from behind and above the boulder.

The fool horse reared, wrenching free and Gus let it go. He slapped it on the rump as it cantered past, desperate to get to Noelle. He lunged, ready to forfeit the kill to relieve the pressure on her neck. He'd lift her and pray her father somehow released the other end of the rope.

The horse charged past, Gus bolted, prepared to lift Noelle—

The rope lay coiled in the mud, and Noelle had toppled in a heap. He reached for her, desperate to shield her with his body. Gunfire echoed. A horse screamed in pain.

A man's body tumbled down the near side of the great boulder, the torch falling with him.

Gus dove for Noelle, only to find Jed had wrested his way free of her insignificant weight. The lunatic clamped one arm around her middle and pressed his blade to her throat.

Around them, the fight continued, but Gus's world narrowed into the finest point: one woman and her single captor.

"You don't want to do this." Gus's breaths came hard and fast, puffs of white in the frigid air.

"You're wrong, Marshal."

He thought about dropping the derringer. He considered taking aim at the very little of Jed not shielded by Noelle's body. He considered pouncing, and beating the life out of the man who dared threaten Noelle's life... and dismissed every one of them just as quick as the ideas struck.

Crimson welled and dribbled from a line on her throat. She winced. Her eyes locked with his, pleading—communicating *something* he couldn't decipher.

"You want to free her, Marshal?" Jed's voice had hardened, reeking with fury and anger. His pitch rose until he'd nearly screamed. "Put that derringer to your head and pull the trigger."

Fourteen

Gus put the barrel to his temple.

Noelle's cry, muffled by her gag, was barely discernible above the cacophony. Another rifle blast, this one close.

He stumbled forward a step, as if struck from behind, a great fist to his shoulder. The blow spun him halfway about, but the derringer remained pressed to the tender flesh at his skull.

He staggered, turned back toward her. Just one more glimpse of her face, just one more fleeting grasp.

One more peek at what should have been.

She fought against Jed's hold. The knife bit deeper into her flesh. Blood dripped down her neck, streaming in earnest.

Cords stood out in Jed's neck, fury stark on his snarled face. "Do it! Pull the trigger, Marshal, or she dies before your eyes, you filthy coward."

Never had he felt so helpless, so emasculated. He'd intentionally walked into Jedediah's grasp, as prepared as he'd known how to be.

He'd failed her.

He'd failed this town, brought the first lawlessness to her peaceable valley.

He regretted *all* of that.

Most of all, he regretted failing Noelle.

This beautiful, vivacious, talented woman who drew likenesses with ease and made him laugh.

He hadn't been able to save her.

The weight of defeat knocked him to his knees. His head swam. He shook it off, forcing the dizziness away.

He drew one last labored breath and prepared to pull the trigger. If this was the only way he had of proving his devotion, his ownership of the doom he'd brought upon Noelle Finlay and her family, he'd do it.

Icy wind cut through him, chilling him to the core. Fear? Maybe, but he figured it was simply the result of staring death in the face while so many regrets remained.

His work wasn't finished.

He might not be able to wrench her free of this madman before he thrust his knife so deep into her throat that he sliced her windpipe and the arteries and she bled out in Gus's arms, but he had to try.

The sounds of gunfire dimmed, and he had the vague sense of a man running through the narrow pass, his rifle drawn. But none of that mattered now. The battle faded.

With the last vestiges of his strength, fighting to stay alert, Gus whipped the pistol from his temple and drew a bead on Jed's forehead. Mere inches from Noelle, but that couldn't be helped. He must stop the madman. This was his *only* choice.

He trembled, shaking, from cold or from terror, he couldn't determine. Praying for an aim true and direct, he pulled the trigger.

Noelle had watched with horror as a bullet had struck Gus in the shoulder. He'd spun like a toy top, the blow nearly knocking him off his feet. She'd screamed and all but blacked out for want of air.

He'd held on, kept going.

Noelle's fingers, numb with cold and deprived of circulation from the ropes binding her wrists, closed around the pistol tucked into Jed's belt. She flinched as the knife he held at her throat cut deeper. Her heart raced and bright spots of light shimmered before her eyes.

She *must* remain conscious.

Her only hope lay with the pistol.

Jed wrenched her closer, his arm locked about her ribs and pinned her hands between their bodies.

The pistol grip stabbed the back of her hand. She'd never get to it now.

Jed's hot breath rasped in her ear. "Do it! Pull the trigger, Marshal, or she dies before your eyes, you filthy coward."

Her heart slammed against her ribs. If only she could scream at Gus to lower that fool derringer, she'd do it. That man deserved a severe talking to.

How could he consider taking his own life?

White hot pain seared from the wound in her neck from Boss's blade. She bit back the urge to cry and twisted, trying for the pistol grip. Jed didn't seem to take notice.

Please, let this be a weapon and not something utterly useless.

She locked her left hand—why couldn't it have been her right?—around the butt.

Jed rocked her body forward.

She grabbed the opportunity and yanked his pistol free of his waistband.

Jed slammed her back against his chest, the knife biting deeper. He'd planted her squarely before him. The monster used her as a shield!

She knew the likelihood of aiming a pistol, behind her back, with her hands bound and wedged so fully between herself and her captor, had very little probability of hitting its mark. She'd likely shoot herself in the spine before she disabled Jed.

But she had to try. And must do it *now*.

Gus stumbled, dropped to one knee, and in so doing, brought the bloodstain from Jed's knife on his side into the firelight. Through all those layers of winter clothing, he bled bright and red and copious in quantity.

He'd lost so much blood! How did he remain conscious?

Still, that pistol pressed to his temple.

If he pulled that trigger, whether intentionally or by accident, she'd kill him herself.

Real fear made her lightheaded. Lights flickered before her eyes.

If Gus shot himself before she managed to disable Boss—how would she live? Did she want to live in a world without Gus?

Bitter cold chilled the hot blood at her neck, and a savage ferocity overtook her person. No outlaw, driven by revenge, would steal her future, take one more life, terrorize her family and her neighbors and her town.

Never again.

She wrestled the pistol, fighting to point the barrel toward Jed. But with him locking her body against his with such unyielding strength, and with the bulk of his coat between them, she couldn't do it. The leverage was off. She hadn't a chance of doing more than grazing his skin.

Frustration welled, spiking her anger.

Her life could *not* end this way.

She would not allow Gus to die in vain.

She was supposed to marry August Rose. They were supposed to live in his house and together, make it a home. She had plans, and those plans didn't include dying for decades to come.

With one last longing glance at the man she loved, wishing she could explain that she'd gladly pass over into death if it meant he'd survive this, she leveraged the pistol the best she could in the cramped space, wrested her body away from Jed's, and pulled the trigger.

The pistol recoiled in Noelle's hand. She felt the slam of the bullet and at her back, Jed spasmed. A spray of warmth and wet *something*— surely blood and body—misted the air at her face.

Had her bullet carved a path from gut to neck?

She would've screamed, had she had breath enough.

As it was, all she could do was fight for air and sift through myriad signals her terrorized brain sent in a tangle.

Had she been shot?

Had she succeeded in shooting Jed?

Her left hand clenched tighter around the pistol. Her ears rang.

She should attempt to fire again.

Her heart galloped at such a dizzying speed, she fought to stay conscious.

Shoot him! She ordered her numb hand to do her bidding.

Jed's fierce lock about her middle lessened,

giving her just enough room to shove the barrel of his pistol deeper into his coat.

She pulled the trigger.

This time, the recoil of the pistol slammed against her back. Pain erupted in her spine and tears flooded her eyes.

Maybe it wasn't the pistol grip... Had she shot herself?

The wash of agony, so intense, told her the bullet meant for her enemy had ricocheted, sliced through her spine and ribs and lungs.

I'm sorry, Gus. So sorry.

Her numb hands fumbled the weapon. She lost her grip. It fell, somewhere, lost if she didn't scramble and relocate it.

Jed seemed stunned. His arm slowly released her and she shimmied away as best she could.

Movement had to mean she'd escaped wounding, didn't it?

Gus dived for her, grabbed her about the arms and hauled her to her feet. Bless him, he fought with the gag until he'd freed her. She gulped air and sobbed.

Shielding her with his wounded body, he hurried her out of the melee, away from waning battle.

"How *could* you?" she demanded of Gus, the moment she could speak.

"How could I what?" he spun her about, and must've sliced through the ropes at her wrists, for the bonds fell away all at once.

"How could you," she still couldn't slow her

breathing, "*consider—*"

He crushed her to him, his lips finding hers and kissing her with the intensity of a man who'd been prepared to die.

She shoved against his chest. The man infuriated her. She wanted to clobber him and kiss him—and clobber him once more for good measure. Had he *no* comprehension what he'd put her through? "You nearly died!"

He ignored her, pressed a hankie to the bloody wound at her neck with such gentleness that tears threatened—again.

Jed. Boss. Her captor, the man who'd tried to slice her neck clean through. She'd killed him. Bile rose in her throat, singeing and burning in its path.

"Is he—dead?" She pulled away from Gus, desperate to ensure this was truly over, that the man behind so many weeks of terror was well and truly dead.

"Yes."

"We should make sure. Before he gets away."

Gus cupped her face, gently turning her attention from the muddy patch of road and squarely upon his face. "He's dead. No question."

"You're sure? I couldn't aim—" she gasped, fighting to draw air and hating herself for panicking, "—not with him holding me so tight."

"I'm sure." He smoothed a stray lock of hair away from her eye. Tenderness and love shone on his face.

She could barely take it all in.

"Don't look."

"How can you be so sure? Plenty of gut-shot men live for days afterward, have more than enough fight left in them to pull a trigger."

"He's dead."

"Oh, for the love of—"

"I shot him, same as you."

Her vehemence trailed off, a puddle of rapidly melting snow. She flashed back, that spray of hot, wet matter. The shudder of Jed's big, hard body. "You shot him—*in the head*?"

Of all the unconscionable, risky, brave and wonderful... her head had been pinned in close proximity to Jed's. If Gus's aim hadn't been straight and true...

Gus stroked her cheek with a tenderness that dissolved her panic, the near miss she'd survived. "You could've killed me."

"Never."

"My head was wedged against his. You took *aim*, Sheriff Rose, and could have killed me." But the surge of dissatisfaction lasted so brief a moment, her accusation held little heat.

He merely lowered his head and kissed her. A sweet, tender, feather-light touch of his warm mouth to hers. A chaste, reverent kiss that nearly undid her.

"Never." The fervency of his whisper seared straight to her heart.

"You'd better tell me, Sheriff, that turning your derringer on yourself was only to buy a few minutes, because if you tell me you intended to shoot yourself, I'm going to—"

Gus pressed a gentle fingertip to her lips. "You can lecture me all you want to, later. For now, I need to see you're safe, then check on the wounded."

Her stomach dropped, as if from a great height.

Luke and Hunter. Gerald, Timothy and Dallas. The deputies. Had hired hands joined them?

"I love you." His whispered pledge, filled with certainty and devotion banished the frigid temperatures and penetrated her heart.

She believed him.

Love welled, overflowed, and presented as tears on her cheeks. "I've loved you, Gus, for a full year."

The grin she loved kicked up the corner of his mouth, and he kissed her once more, quickly. "I think I could get used to hearing that from you, lady."

He tried to seclude her at the far edge of the bend in the road, upon his own mount, but she wouldn't have any of that. "Every time I let you out of my sight, Sheriff, you end up almost dead. Don't argue with me. You need someone to look after you."

Fifteen

Two days later, the bodies of the dead gang members were displayed. Among them, the traitorous Clifford Cox—*if* that was the name his mama had given him.

Seven open caskets reclined against the front wall of the Sheriff's Office.

A morbid tradition, but tradition it was, and served a few significant purposes.

First, positive proof their reign of terror had come to an abrupt end.

Second, the grizzly sight discouraged young men from romanticizing a life of crime.

Third, townsfolk could see for themselves that the law had, indeed, done something.

Gus still found the practice distasteful.

In the end, two bandits had survived, though seriously wounded. Both were secured behind iron bars, healing and awaiting the arrival of a pair of U.S. Marshals to transfer them to the State Penitentiary in Cañon City.

Gus had seen to it they'd had the best of treatment from Doc Cheney and regular visits thereafter. The two varmints would regain their health, if Gus had any say in the matter. They'd stand up when sentenced in a court of law. And they'd serve their time.

Death would be easier than they deserved.

Everyone from the outlying areas had joined the folks who lived in town, congregating on the boardwalk and crowded on the snow-packed street, stretching for a full block in either direction from the jail-house. A few inventive souls had filled the buildings across the street, opened windows to the bitter chill and leaned out for a good view. A few rapscallion young men had climbed onto the icy roofs.

Fools. No news was worth a broken neck.

Gus stood atop a barrel to better see over the crowd, and to ensure they heard him. So many faces that had held hostility at the last town meeting in the Finlay home responded to him now as if he'd singlehandedly removed the threat from their midst.

Though they'd believed him incompetent mere days ago, they now thought him invincible. A hero.

The mood that Monday morning was darn

near as jubilant as it'd been last Independence Day when the town had celebrated with a parade and dancing.

The only dark spot in the festivities were the two members of Noelle's family that hadn't come into town.

He swallowed against the grief rising in his throat and forced those thoughts away—there wasn't a blasted thing he could do about it now.

So, back to the Fourth of July his thoughts scurried.

'Course, it'd been hot as the dickens on Independence Day, and this morning, the cold bit straight through his greatcoat, and every extra layer, including his Union suit.

He couldn't wait to get this meeting over with. He had a hot cup of Arbuckle's waiting on him, and a comfortable chair beside the stove.

"Quiet down." He raised an arm, signaling for their attention. He couldn't help but smile. Coming through on the other side felt far too good.

Everybody ignored him. Instead of hushing up, some whistled, and others cheered. Ladies waved their handkerchiefs and men twirled their hats. Muffled applause—too cold to go without gloves, mittens, or muffs—filled in the background.

Finally, *finally*, the revelry quieted.

The sun shone bright from a near-cloudless winter sky, reflecting brilliantly off the blanket of snow. He squinted, taking in the hundreds of faces—people he knew well and some he didn't. He was glad to see Mrs. Boczowski standing midst a circle of her friends, women who'd ensured she had clothing, shelter, food, and hearth. She'd be all right.

Right in front of him, the Finlay family had taken the place of honor, his beautiful Noelle close enough to touch, and he ached to do just that. She wore a heavy, long winter cloak that covered her from nape to heel.

He'd helped her into that cloak, right after he'd seen for himself that the wound on her neck had begun to close with the help of twenty tidy stitches.

In comparison, his own injuries were too minor to mention. What was a nick to the shoulder or scrape to the ribs when set side-by-side with a knife wound to the neck?

Noelle's bandage was out of sight beneath her high-collared cloak, but he'd never forget it was there.

Sure as her skin would scar as it healed, some memories would never fade.

He'd be reminded every day of his life how close he'd come to losing her. Not something a man could contemplate for long without losing his sanity.

He shook off the lingering regrets as the joyous mood quieted. All eyes had turned to him.

He let a deep breath go, wishing all the tension away with it. The puff of breath, white in the bitter cold, reminded him how blessedly alive he was.

"Seven men," he shouted, enunciating with

care, "of the Ruffian Gang are dead."

The announcement deserved solemnity—but it was also a cause for jubilation. The crowd erupted with more applause, whistles, and cheers than he thought possible from several hundred folk. Their response cheered him and he couldn't help but grin. This day had been long in coming.

He gestured for silence, and once the cacophony had quieted enough, he continued with more of what they already knew. "The two remaining marauders await justice in the jail."

Too bad the double-crossing Cliff Cox had been fatally wounded. The traitor had died within minutes of Gus finding him. He would've preferred to have seen Cliff stand before the judge, the filth of his crimes bared before the law. Gus would have built the gallows with his own two hands and celebrated the day Cliff hanged.

But it wasn't to be.

"Jedediah Smythe, the man his gang called 'Boss,' is among the dead." He paused in his announcement and sought Noelle's upturned face so near. His heart swelled with the odd, disquieting combination of love and panic he'd come to associate with her.

The brave, resourceful, fool woman had freed herself. She hadn't truly needed his kill shot after all.

Doc Cheney had said so. Her first shot to Smythe's gut had lodged in his chest, likely piercing his lung and nicking the heart. He'd have died from that first desperate shot.

Every time he replayed that brief moment, he saw Noelle's beautiful face.

He'd turned his derringer from his own temple to fire upon Jed Smythe. Without pausing to slow his breathing, without excruciating aim, without waiting for absolute stillness between beats of his own heart.

Noelle's beautiful face. Mere inches from the center of Smythe's forehead.

He wanted to vomit.

It all could have gone desperately wrong, so fast. He'd never forget. Never. As long as he lived.

"Rumors," he bellowed, forcing his emotions deep so they couldn't wobble his voice, "abound, so I'm here to set them straight."

The crowd had remained quiet. Only the cries of a few babies, chatter of young children upon their fathers' shoulders, and fussing of little ones were heard.

The time had come to confess all. His shame, regret, and ownership of the whole mess.

The good people of Mountain Home deserved to know.

Somehow, his gaze landed on Sheriff Liam Talmadge, the old man who'd retired not long after Gus had taken a deputy position with him. Gus had come to town, with high hopes.

Instead, he'd brought evil upon the heads of these good people.

"I've heard tell," he continued, "the Ruffian Gang descended upon Mountain Home for this reason or for that, but the truth is this: Jedediah

Smythe built his gang from the dregs of men. He came to Mountain Home hunting *me*."

A few murmurs spouted in little pockets of disturbance. Women's bonnets rippled in the crowd as wives turned to husbands.

He had to voice the truth. Let them vote. Let them decide.

He held up a hand, gesturing for silence. "I made my share of enemies in Connecticut, as a U.S. Marshal, guarding and protecting federal judges. One of those many enemies was Jedediah Smythe—an attorney."

Surprise punctuated their mutterings, giving rise and excitement to the ripple of conversation scattering throughout the crowd.

A stiff, chilly wind skittered through, but Gus barely acknowledged it.

He pressed on. "One of Smythe's clients, whom I saw imprisoned for crimes against a federal judge, happened to be his half-brother. For reasons I cannot fathom, Smythe blamed me for that criminal's death while incarcerated."

He sighed. This wouldn't be easy. Truth be told, the only easy day had been yesterday. "Jed Smythe is not my only enemy." He paused, giving them time to recognize the weight of this disclosure. "Residents, fine people of Mountain Home—if he followed me here, others will also."

He let that sink in, drew a deep breath, then two. Truth of that statement registered on many faces. More men than he'd counted on looked away, hiding their expressions behind brims of their hats. Women who'd been smiling not five minutes before now turned their attention to their little ones.

Truth was a hard pill to swallow.

Having a former United States Marshal as their Sheriff wasn't so illustrious and wonderful. They'd all fully supported Talmadge's retirement a year ago, but that had been before they'd seen the elephant, so to speak.

Despite the uncomfortable shifting of the crowd up and down the street, his attention focused on Noelle, her eyes bright with unshed tears. She reached for him.

She closed her gloved fingers around his, lending him strength he didn't deserve. Her affection, her very life lent him strength to say what he must. He covered their joined hands, beyond grateful for this strong woman's support. She wanted him.

Him.

With his broken-down, hand-me-down heart. With his lawman's past, the likelihood of others coming and wreaking more of the same havoc.

She still wanted a life with him.

Even with her father laid up in his bed, suffering pain of a broken arm because he'd followed Gus into the fray to rescue his daughter. Because her papa had dared defy the villains who hated Gus. The villains who'd forced him to hold the hanging rope taut.

She wanted him anyway.

Even though her elder brother, Luke, had

taken a bullet in the thigh, and lay at home convalescing. Gus had witnessed the agony of that slug's removal, the copious blood lost, the pain Luke had endured, and the abundance of Effie's tears.

He'd known then, in the Finlay kitchen, that his heart was well and truly Noelle's. Any hold Effie had held over him belonged fully in his past. Yes, he cared about her. She was part of the Finlay family, a chapter from his youth, a friend.

Noelle had set him free.

A man could not recognize the weight of a life-altering miracle and hesitate to act accordingly.

He'd do the right thing.

Both for the town that relied on him for law and order, and for the gal his one-woman heart had chosen.

A squeeze to her fingers, strong and certain, cradled within his own, and he felt more grounded, more certain than ever.

"By the grace of God, we lost not a single soul." He still couldn't believe the odds had been wholly in their favor. "Every loss of life was among our enemies."

He scanned their faces, noting most had returned their attention to him in full. "I cannot guarantee those odds next time. I'm astonished we came through with only two wounded—and while Noelle's father and brother are wounded, they have an excellent chance of survival. Pray for them."

Murmurs skittered through the crowd. It was old news, the status of Phil and Luke. Word like that—and good news of no deaths among their own—traveled fast, right along with the word of a town meeting and seeing the villains laid out. Everybody knew details before they'd arrived this morning.

But he had news they couldn't already know, because he'd told no one. Yet.

"In light of the terrors visited upon this valley and its residents, I resign as Sheriff of Mountain Home."

He'd barely announced 'resign' when the hubbub escalated. Cries of "no!" mingled with a burble of murmurs so intense no one could've heard him, even if he'd tried. So he waited.

And stood, in amazement, at the negative response from the crowd. They didn't like his intention to resign.

He glanced at Noelle. Her expression evidenced love, respect, and trust. This amazing woman, he believed, would follow him, no matter where he went.

Joy swelled.

Regardless of what happened with his employment, the big, empty house few could afford to buy from him, he'd be perfectly O.K. as long as Noelle was at his side.

"You can't resign!" This from old Liam Talmadge, who'd last worn the badge. "Your petition is denied."

A dozen men bellowed their affirmative, "I second the motion."

The two deputies, Murphy and Dillinger,

standing together on the boardwalk off to the side bellowed, "we second the motion too!"

"The only way," Talmadge yelled, "to leave the post of Sheriff of Mountain Home, is to die wearing the badge, or find someone better qualified and much younger to pass it on to."

Chuckles danced among the throng. Applause peppered the air. Ladies waved their hankies.

"You ain't leavin, son, 'til you find someone better for the job than yourself." Talmadge thumped his cane on the boardwalk beneath his feet. "If you want out, I suggest you start lookin' for a replacement."

Gus couldn't help it—he laughed. He'd been prepared for the worst, to be run out of town on a rail, a posse of angry residents intent on doing him harm close behind.

He'd been the reason for the raids, after all. *The* reason Mrs. Boczowski's home had burned to the ground. *The* reason Elias Kennedy's milk cow had been slaughtered.

Having spent most of his savings on that big, fancy house the mayor had sold him, he didn't have the money to compensate those folks.

Maybe he ought to give his house to Mrs. Boczowski. The big, empty mansion would more than compensate—he hoped—for her burned-out cabin and lost possessions.

Drawn to Noelle, he sought her take on all this. Her smile, so bright, so filled with joy and contentment, sealed up the cracks in his heart and applied relieving salve to his smarting pride.

"All in favor," Mayor Abbot hollered, from his perch on a wagon bed across the street, "of *denying* Sheriff Rose's resignation, say aye!"

A tumult of *ayes* swept through the crowd with the rumble of thunder.

Emotion rose so thick, so intense, Gus nearly lost his lid. Men wearing tin stars did *not* weep like little girls.

"Those opposed to denying the resignation, say nay." Abbot's tone of voice held a double-dose of accusation for any who'd dare send their lawman-hero skedaddling.

More than a few men replied with a vehement, "Nay!"

"Duly noted," the mayor stated. "The ayes have it."

More applause, cheers, and whistles. Gus laughed—so stunned by the overwhelming show of support, now that folks understood what having him around meant.

"August Rose," Mayor Abbot intoned, "your petition to resign from your post as Sheriff of Mountain Home, Colorado, is hereby denied."

Sixteen

On Christmas Eve, Gus knocked on the Finlay's front door. Midday sunlight filtered through the snowfall, a portent of lousy roads on his way home, so he'd tucked Beau away in the barn.

With luck, he'd arrived early enough he wouldn't intrude on everything Christmas.

Even though Noelle had invited him to join the family, he couldn't see himself pretending to enjoy it.

August Rose and Christmas didn't get along.

"You're staying for Christmas," Caroline Finlay informed Gus when she answered the door, "and that's final."

Not the quick in-and-out visit Gus had planned on, but by the light dancing in his would-be mother-in-law's eyes, he recognized her genuine affection for him.

"Thank you, Mrs. Finlay."

"You're to call me Mother. Or Mama if you're particularly affectionate."

"Yes, ma'am."

"Are you mumbling, son? You must learn to pronounce your words clearly. *Mother.*" Her grin nearly had him chuckling. "Try again."

"Mother."

"Much better."

He'd only stopped by long enough to check on Noelle's father and Luke. He'd heard Luke had taken ill with a high fever. He'd needed to see for himself.

Thank God, the rumors had been exaggerated. Yes, Luke had suffered a fever, but nothing more than what Doc assured was therapeutic. Luke was on the mend, already up and about, a week after the shoot-out.

Phil Finlay would take longer to heal. It'd been a bad break and the man might never have full use of his arm again.

Meeting the older man's gaze, seeing the agony of the broken bone in his eyes, knowing he'd brought on the injury by not insisting he stay behind, was painful.

He cleared his throat. "Yes ma'am."

"Take off your coat right now. Get yourself into the parlor. It's time to open our gifts."

Panic seized him hard.

Christmas. And presents. He'd never had anyone to buy for, and received so few gifts on the holiday throughout his life, it had never occurred to him to think about it.

Even for Noelle.

He bit back a curse. None of this was going well. He remembered why he detested Christmas. This was *not* his holiday.

The house was filled to capacity. Every married sibling had come home for Christmas with his or her spouse and children. The house smelled wonderful. Roasting ham, potatoes, something laced with cinnamon and sugar.

It smelled like a real home.

Nothing like his empty, cavernous, dusty house.

He really ought to sell the monstrosity. Or marry Noelle and fill the house with children, one by one.

He'd wanted a family when he'd bought the house...though he'd thought he wanted a family with Effie.

Funny, to look back on that dream, and realize what he'd desperately wanted—Effie as his bride—was no longer the dream he desired.

Now, all he wanted was for Noelle to accept him, wed him, and make their house a home.

She knew all about real families. She'd grown up with an abundance of love, siblings, laughter, and parents who'd shown her by example what it meant to be part of a family.

She'd know exactly what that big house needed. If she'd have him, she'd turn his house into a home.

He found himself ushered into the crowded parlor, surrounded by every last Finlay. To his surprise, he found it blissfully sweet.

He sought and found Noelle, sitting on a kitchen chair set near to her father's side. The old man had his broken arm elevated on pillows as he reclined on a sofa.

Noelle's smile warmed him clear though. She looked radiant in a deep purple silk blouse, a cameo brooch at her throat, closing a little stand-up collar that covered her injury. He'd never seen this fancy blouse before, and he found he didn't want to look away.

Her eyes shone with welcome.

"Come," she said, "sit by Papa." She slid down a seat and patted the chair she'd just vacated. Pearl ear bobs swayed with her movement, catching his eye and holding his attention.

Or maybe his attention was merely captivated by everything Noelle.

Heat flushed through his innards—today was her birthday!—why hadn't he remembered?

He'd make a horrid mess of things...

She patted the chair once more. He obeyed this time, finding the wood warm with the heat of her body. The press of her shoulder against his and the comfort of her little hand tucked within his felt like the warmest of hellos.

A man could get used to this.

Would she want to become used to him?

"Happy birthday," he whispered near her ear. She smelled good. Floral fragrance and spice—had she been baking?

"Thank you."

Mr. Finlay had called the family to order before Gus noticed no gaily wrapped gifts beneath or on the tree. The long line of stockings tacked to the mantle seemed empty. He glanced at Noelle, curious.

She simply smiled.

What, did they have someone dressed up to play jolly old St. Nicholas, ready to bound in with a sack of gifts for the little ones?

"Mother," Phil Finlay directed from his repose on the sofa, "I need your help this year. You present the gifts, will you?"

Gus soon realized each stocking contained notes, folded letters, even scraps of paper with childish handwriting upon them. Messages of love, affection, promises of time to be spent together doing all those things real families did.

By the time the strangely reverent experience had passed through three-fourths of the family, Gus was startled to hear Noelle's mother call *his* name.

He startled and instinctively tossed up two hands to ward Caroline off.

Oh, no. He hadn't participated in this...hadn't put a single note in anyone's stocking. No way would he be able to read words of kindness from these good people and keep his composure.

Lawmen don't shed tears, even on Christmas.

"August Rose." Caroline brought him a bright red stocking, trimmed in white hand-tatted lace at the cuff. It looked new, fresh, as if she'd just sewn it.

Why would she do a thing like that?

His name had been embroidered along the sweep of what would've been the toe in a real stocking. His throat closed with an emotion he couldn't identify and he glanced in panic from Noelle to her mother to Luke.

Of all people, *why* Luke?

Noelle put a hand on his shoulder and leaned close to whisper. "Go ahead. You don't have to read aloud if you don't want to."

Caroline pushed the beautiful handiwork into his hands. He ran callused fingers over the lace, a ridiculous gesture as his dry, rough fingers caught on the tatting and silk.

His heart skipped a beat, slammed hard against his healing ribs, and he had a sudden urge to bolt for the door.

What was he doing here?

Why had he thought he could borrow this family, even for the afternoon?

Mere seconds had passed, but he felt all eyes on him, and this proved far harder than standing up to the entire town had been.

Noelle, bless her, saw right through him, for she reached for the mouth of the stocking and pulled out a bit of paper. She turned it right-side up and held it between them, inviting Gus to read along with her.

This note was scrawled in a child's hand, brief, poignant. "Thank you for protecting Auntie

Noelle." It was signed *Clara,* and Gus had to wonder which of the cherubs, sitting upon the floor, answered to Clara.

Noelle slipped her arm through his, snuggled against him, and carefully pointed out a little girl of maybe seven years. "That's beautiful, Clara. Thank you."

Maybe this wasn't so hard. Gus let out a breath. He could do this.

One by one, he read notes penned by almost all members of the family. When, exactly, had they determined to include him in this family tradition?

The realization humbled him, and made him wonder at their overall assumption that he and Noelle were a certainty, all tied up with a bright red Christmas bow.

He hadn't proposed marriage.

Yet.

But he intended to.

Now that he knew he'd well and certain lost his heart to her, that *she* was his future—*if* she'd have a man ten years her senior—what choice did he have?

He wanted this woman by his side, in his life, in his bed, as the mother of his children. He wanted her to complete him.

She already had.

All he needed now was to put a ring on her finger and officially make it so.

Noelle pulled out another note, this one on lovely rose-colored stationery and folded in thirds. "From me."

Her smile arrowed straight for his heart. He trembled, a most unmanly reaction, as he unfolded her letter and took in the exquisitely formed penmanship, the words she'd formed on paper, words he could keep and cherish always.

My dearest Gus,

You've won the privilege of hearing my entire story. From the beginning. You're the only man I want to share my story with, as I trust you with the information. I also know your regard for my parents won't change, regardless of things that transpired two decades past.

I told you that if I ever shared the details, which I will, the moment we're alone and I can explain in person, this means you're mine.

Merry Christmas, my love.

Noelle

Gus waited, silent, the import of her letter resting warm upon his heart. In that moment, his love for Noelle outgrew its barrel and overflowed. He'd simply have to find a way to grow a bigger heart.

He didn't see any other solution.

As it was, he loved this woman more every day.

He'd yet to see the Finlays respond with more than a thank you, the touch of a hand upon a shoulder, a hug between sisters.

But love for Noelle, who'd just opened her arms and her heart as wide as they'd go and welcomed him home, wouldn't be denied. He set the precious letter on his knee, took her face in his hands, awed and humbled by the love he witnessed in her honey-brown eyes.

"Merry Christmas," he whispered.

"Merry Christmas."

He kissed her. Sweet and pure and fit for the whole family to witness—if she was his bride-to-be, which, of course, she was.

It wasn't until she'd pulled away and rested her cheek upon his shoulder that Gus realized his first love, Effie, sat across the room, holding her husband's hand.

Nothing had ever felt quite so right.

The family—quite out of character for the reverence of their traditional gift-giving—erupted into applause.

Brothers whistled. A couple little girls pushed to their feet and jumped up and down with the buoyancy only toddlers had. Caroline touched her fingertips to her eyes, blotting away a tear or two.

Noelle slipped her hands into the curls in his over-long hair. Her soft smile made him reconsider.

Perhaps he liked Christmas.

With her, he imagined, he might learn to like Christmas a great deal.

Please *share* this book with a friend.
Paperbacks are easy to lend.

Please *recommend* this book.
Please share your thoughts on this book with friends.

Please post a *review.*
Reviews from readers make all the difference to those browsing and buying, as well as to writers. Please take a moment and leave an honest review. One short sentence will do.

To Review *The Marshal's Surrender* Online:

One Quick Click =
one page links you to all review sites
(stores where you might have purchased this title, and exclusive review sites like Goodreads and BookBub).

Simply type in:

www.kristinholt.com/review-the-marshals-surrender

(not case-sensitive, but dashes/hyphens are required)

Or scan the QR code.

Keep turning pages for:

Noelle promised Gus more information... page 212

Dear Reader (historical background details about this novel).... page 208

Great Grandma Sorenson's Chicken and Dumplings Recipe... page 216

Note: throughout the rest of my Dear Reader section, all bold-face words or phrases are links in the kindle edition—and connect to a wealth of background and historical information. If you're interested, please visit

www.kristinholt.com/history-the-marshals-surrender *(or scan the QR code)*

to view this same content <u>with clickable links</u>.

The Marshal's Surrender—"Gus's Story"—has been

simmering on the back burner for more than two years. The tentative title began as *A Christmas Courtship*, then morphed to *The Sheriff's Surrender*, and eventually became the best-fitting (IMHO) *The Marshal's Surrender*.

Why did it have to cook "for a month of Sundays"?

Ummm.....?

Perhaps my best answer is a combination of what I suspect and what I know.

First, I suspect this book was harder to write than many of my previous efforts. "Harder" in the sense that many of the issues both Gus and Noelle combat in order to feel worthy of love and dare take the risk with each other, hoping that their relationship just might grow roots and last are more my own than previous characters. You could say much of my heart is in this story.

Secondly, I know many readers are less enamored of "Christmas Stories" than I am. I could happily read Christmas-set stories at least every-other-title. Something about Christmas Romances fill my heart with contentment—just what sweet western historical romance should do (once the characters battle **through their challenges**, difficulties, grow, learn, and commit of course). **Christmas-themed romances** tend to have elements of family, trust, honor, giving, awareness of the needs of others, faith and so much more. Those themes always appeal to me, set at Christmastime or not.

When all is said and done, I'm so pleased to

finally have **The Marshal's Surrender** ready to share with you.

So, not to change topics suddenly or anything... but <u>is Marshal spelled with one L, or Marshall, with two</u>? According to **Merriam-Webster, marshal** <u>is correct</u> (in American English), and a variant spelling (less commonly) is marshall. The **U.S. Marshals Service** website spells their name with one L. Given Gus served as a U.S. Marshal, it made sense to follow their lead.

Apparently a double-l is used in some European countries. Wikipedia gives an answer that disagrees with most online dictionaries (so does this mean we don't trust Wikipedia?). Ultimately, Marshall is the more common spelling of surnames, and either spelling is passable when referencing the law enforcement role. I'm writing several brief **blog articles specifically about the fascinating history of the U.S. Marshals**. I hope you'll stop by and enjoy these tidbits from American history that set the stage for Gus's law enforcement experience prior to Mountain Home and his job as Sheriff. You'll find the details within articles on **www.KristinHolt.com**.

In December 2016, I gave a shorter novella as a gift to readers. **This Noelle** is a prequel of sorts to the **Holidays in Mountain Home Series** (book #0.5) that will be <u>available only as a gift to subscribers to my newsletter</u> (update: the paperback edition is for sale, and the kindle edition remains my gift to subscribers) Why? Because I genuinely want to give generously to my readers.

This story, set in Mountain Home, Colorado in 1881, is about 20 years earlier than the other **4 numbered books in the series**, and 1 ½ years after the unnumbered novella connected to the series—***Courting Miss Cartwright***. All you have to do to add yourself to my holiday gift-giving list is to sign up for my once-in-a-while newsletter (I promise to safeguard your email address, never share/rent/give/disclose/sell it to anyone else, and to send newsletters only when I have something to say I think you might like to hear. Every emailed newsletter has an "unsubscribe" link so it's easy to disconnect if you don't want to hear from me anymore.

I'm toying with the idea of committing to a new, available-only-to-my-newsletter subscribers novella for each and every upcoming Christmas. Would you like that? Drop me a note through my website (**www.KristinHolt.com/contact-kristin**), or send me a direct email if you prefer (Kristin@KristinHolt.com).

Note: Kristin is e-free!

I enjoy hearing from readers and do my best to respond to every last (reasonable) email from readers. So, if you have feedback, ideas, an answer to my question (about an annual holiday gift through my newsletter), questions (upcoming book releases, for example), or just want to say hi, please contact me. I'll enjoy hearing from you.

Oh—if you're reading this well past December 2016, please know that ***This Noelle*** will be available somewhere. If it's no longer the exclusive gift to newsletter subscribers, I've probably made it available elsewhere. Check out my **Books** (www.KristinHolt.com/books) page on my website for links to all of my titles.

What about Noelle's secret, the secret she promised to share with Gus? Something about her <u>*mother*</u>*?*

Find out in

This Noelle

www.kristinholt.com/book-description-this-noelle

(address is not case-sensitive, but dashes (hyphens) are required)
Or scan this QR code:

Note: Noelle, Gus's bride in *The Marshal's Surrender*, is a new baby and the namesake of *This Noelle*. As books are loosely connected, you're welcome to read in any order.

If you enjoyed ***The Marshal's Surrender*** or other books I've written, you might want to bookmark my **Books** page and check back often. I have several books coming out right after these two

Christmas titles. ***Pleasance's First Love*** (Book #3 in *Six Brides for Six Gideons* AND #6 in a new multi-author series *Grandma's Wedding Quilts*) debuts on January 13, 2017. ***Gunsmoke and Gingham***, a multi-author boxed set containing my title, ***The Gunsmith's Bride***, will publish on February 1, 2017. And on February 24, 2017, Mirror Press (who published ***Mail Order Bride Collection: A Timeless Romance Anthology***—containing my title, ***WANTED: Midwife Bride***—and made the USA Today Bestseller List!) brings you my title, ***Sophia's Leap-Year Courtship***. All five of these titles are NEW, never-before released, and will hopefully bring you as much enjoyment reading them as I had in writing them.

Wishing you and yours a most joyful holiday season. May the light of Christmas last a little longer in your heart this year.

With warmest appreciation,

Kristin

In Chronological Order:

Courting Miss Cartwright (Rocky & Felicity), **1879**
Book 5, Founder's Day NOVELLA

This Noelle (Phil & Caroline), **1881**
Prequel: Book 0.5, Christmas NOVELLA

The Gunsmith's Bride (Morgan & Elizabeth), **1885**
Book 6, Independence Day NOVELLA

Unmistakably Yours (Hank & Jane, Oscar & Ina), **1887**
Book 8, Thanksgiving NOVEL

Home for Christmas (Hunter & Miranda), **1898**
Book 1, Christmas NOVELLA

Maybe This Christmas (Luke & Effie), **1899**
Book 2, Christmas NOVELLA

The Witching Eve (Gus & Noelle), **1900**
Title 7, Halloween SHORT STORY

The Marshal's Surrender (Gus & Noelle), **1900**
Book 3, Christmas NOVEL

The Drifter's Proposal (Malloy & Adaline), **1900**
Book 4, Christmas NOVELLA

http://www.kristinholt.com/holidays-in-

mountain-home-series

P.S. to find my page:

www.kristinholt.com/holidays-in-mountain-home-series

more quickly, see:

http://bit.ly/2A754ZY
(case sensitive)

or scan this code:

GREAT GRANDMA SORENSON'S
Chicken & Dumplings

from Kristin Holt

My great grandma was born in 1896. While this recipe is attributed to her, family lore is she made chicken and dumplings the way her mother did... so this recipe is *an oldie and a goodie.* I'll provide the recipe in the old-fashioned "down-home" way, then with modern day modifications that make preparing this pioneer favorite much easier.

This recipe is easily adjusted to the size/appetite of your family. Make as small or as large a pot as you wish, with the ratio of chicken to vegetables that you prefer.

First, make the soup ~

INGREDIENTS

1 whole chicken (cleaned, bled), boiled and deboned— do *not* discard the stock!
2 quarts stock from simmering the chicken, strained if you wish
Salt and pepper to taste
7 to 8 sliced carrots
5 to 6 potatoes, cubed (if soup isn't soup without potatoes...grandma left them out)

DIRECTIONS:

1. Boil chicken. Discard liquid, skin, and bones. Cut cooked chicken into bite-sized pieces.
2. Heat broth with vegetables and pieces of chicken until it comes to a boil.
3. Meanwhile, *prepare dumplings*.

WHOLE POT
(SERVES 8 TO 10):
INGREDIENTS:

½ cup real dairy butter
1 ½ cups milk
1 ¾ cups flour
3 eggs
3 Tbsp. sugar

SMALL POT
(SERVES 3 TO 4):
INGREDIENTS:

3 Tbsp. real dairy butter
½ cup milk
Heaping ½ cup flour
1 egg
1 Tbsp. sugar

DIRECTIONS:

1. Melt butter in a frying pan. Remove pan from heat. Stir in milk and flour until it forms a paste. Return to heat and fry dough until it turns translucent and opaque.
2. Crack egg(s) into mixing bowl. Add sugar. Add milk/flour mixture. With an electric mixer (I'm sure grandma whipped it with a wooden spoon), whip all ingredients together until smooth.
3. Drop dumplings by tablespoonfuls into boiling soup in an even single layer across surface.
4. Boil soup for 10 minutes with lid on. Uncover and boil another 10 minutes without lid.

SUBSTITUTIONS FOR A Modern Cook

- Use 1 whole stewing chicken, or even easier, IQF (Individually Quick Frozen) chicken breasts, OR a rotisserie chicken, deboned.
- Substitute canned chicken broth, or better yet *Better Than Bouillon*
- Peeled, washed baby carrots

Books by Kristin Holt

www.KristinHolt.com/books

And while you're there, please sign up for her newsletter. *Be the first to hear about new releases, sales, and subscriber-only extras.*

Learn more about Kristin Holt's Series:

THE HUSBAND-MAKER TRILOGY

PROSPERITY'S MAIL ORDER BRIDES

SIX BRIDES FOR SIX GIDEONS

HOLIDAYS IN MOUNTAIN HOME

And **collaborative works**

USA TODAY Bestselling Author

KRISTIN HOLT

Hi! I'm Kristin Holt, *USA Today* bestselling author of Sweet Romances (G- and PG-rated) set in the Victorian American West.

While secular in nature, my titles are "Appropriate for All Audiences" and appeal to selective readers and fans of Christian and Inspirational historical romance.

I write frequent articles (or *view recent posts easily* on my Home Page, www.KristinHolt.com,

scroll down) about the **nineteenth century American west—every subject of possible interest to readers**, amateur historians, authors...as all of these tidbits surfaced while researching for my books. I also blog monthly at *Sweet Americana Sweethearts* and *Sweet Romance Reads*. You'll find links to my blog posts and a wealth of information on my website:
www.KristinHolt.com
I love to hear from readers! Please drop me a note:
www.KristinHolt.com/contact-kristin
(Kristin is e-free.)

Or find me on Facebook:
www.facebook.com/KristinHoltSweetVicto rianWesternRomance/ *(Kristin is e-free)*

You're invited to join a fantastic Facebook group for authors and readers of Western Historical Romances (of all heat levels), Pioneer Hearts.
www.Facebook.com/groups/pioneerhearts

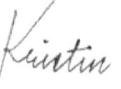